THE
YAKUZA PATH
SERIES

AMY TAS

ONE
THOUSAND
CRANES

ACKNOWLEDGEMENTS

• • •

Thank you to my husband and family, without whose love and support this book would probably not be here. Lorelai, who was a constant cheerleader even when I complained to her about various bookish things. The other awesome people who read the book at various drafts, Nell Iris, Nicky Spencer, Anne Raven, and Lou. My wonderful reader Lauren Handy and her cat, Milly, were the lucky winners to become immortal. Thanks!

Finally, you. Thanks for giving my book a try.

The Yakuza Path: One Thousand Cranes

© 2017 Amy Tasukada

Cover design by Natasha Snow
Print interior and typesetting by Write Dream Repeat Book Design

ISBN Paper: 978-1-948361-01-9

This is a work of fiction. Any similarity between the characters and situations within its pages and places or persons, living or dead, is unintentional and co-incidental.

CHAPTER 01

...

"CONGRATULATIONS!"

Aki Hisona clinked his beer glass against the others, then pretended to drink. His best friends, Shoda and Fuse, chugged theirs down, while Fuse's date took a dainty sip. A waiter came by and exchanged their empty glasses for new.

It had already been a long night of barhopping, but since Aki's promotion, he hadn't been able to spend time with his friends. Even if they all lived in the Kyoto yakuza headquarters, Aki's new rank in the mob made socialization harder than folding origami paper into a dragon.

A woman slinked over to their table. Her long curly hair bounced as much as her breasts with each black high-heeled step.

"Who's the man of the hour?" she asked.

Fuse wrapped his arm around his date. Though, it wouldn't be the first time Fuse went home with more than one woman.

"He's the one." Fuse pointed to Aki.

She pulled a chair beside Aki. "What position are you in now?"

"Secretary to Godfather Murata." Shoda pushed one long bang out of his eye. "Can you believe it? He didn't even have to finish his apprenticeship, and now he answers phones and makes tea all day."

Fuse rolled his eyes. "Come on. You know he has to deal with Father Murata fucking him across the nearest surface whenever he wants."

Aki pressed his lips together. "Murata—"

"It's true, then? The head of the Matsukawa yakuza likes men?" the woman asked.

Fuse laughed. "That's not much of a secret, lady."

Aki took a gulp of his beer, letting the bitter taste wash away what he wanted to say. Nao Murata hadn't bent him across any surface. It had all been faked, and the only thing Nao had allowed to pass between them had been a hasty kiss, for which he later apologized. Aki curled his toes. Just thinking about it made him wish all the rumors about them were true.

"I'm sure it won't be too long before we're all drinking into the morning celebrating both of your promotions," Aki said. "To your future promotions."

Aki's muscles tightened under Fuse's glare, even if he tried to hide it by planting another kiss on his date's lips. But Fuse finally held up his glass to the toast and clinked it with the others.

Aki chugged what remained of his beer, knowing better than to leave any after the toast.

Fuse and Shoda had joined the Matsukawa a few months before Aki. He looked to them as older brothers, but with the promotion, Aki vastly outranked them. Of course they'd be agitated with the situation, but Aki wouldn't let it ruin their friendship. The members of the Matsukawa were the only family he had.

"Perhaps I can persuade Father Murata to move back the apprenticeship six months," Aki said.

Shoda leaned back in his chair. "You got him wrapped around your finger, eh?"

The foam bubbles on Aki's glass clustered together as they slid down. If he had Nao wrapped around his finger, Aki wouldn't have to remember to breathe around him.

"Still, congratulations, babe. You must be making the big bucks now." The woman beside Aki smiled and playfully rubbed his arm. "Aren't you hot with those long sleeves?"

Aki turned away and tugged his shirtsleeve back down. Aki had mastered painting a flawless complexion and wore long sleeves so he didn't have to explain his vitiligo, and she was trying to expose it. She'd have better luck doubling with Fuse than him.

"Fuse, what were you saying about that fishmonger from a few days ago?" Aki changed the subject.

"It's that new apprentice who's a fucking moron. He doesn't know not to put the thumb on the scales with the Matsukawa or else we might just chop them off. First, I'm like 'is that really the price?' and he's all 'yeah, that's the price.' I asked him one more time to be sure, but still the same fucking price.

"What am I supposed to do? If I pay for the fish, then I get home and everyone thinks I stole the money. I don't want to piss off Father Murata. The guy's fucking crazy."

"You gotta keep quiet around him. Give him no good reason to snap like he did last time with you." Shoda leaned back. "It's easy to play the game."

"We can't all be the golden boy of the April recruits."

"Do what everyone says. It's not hard."

"Don't worry. It's the fucking last time I open my mouth around Father Murata. He'd probably snap my neck in half if he thought I got out of line again."

As godfather to the Matsukawa, Nao Murata demanded loyalty and for the family members to know their place in the hierarchy. So, of course, when Fuse had stepped out of line, Nao not only had to remind Fuse of his place, but also show the other recruits such behavior was not acceptable. Fuse's bashed ego made it impossible for him to see the logic in the punishment Nao delivered. Aki shook his head; the grudge Fuse had would get him into trouble one day.

"The fish bastard had to learn not to mess with a Matsukawa," Fuse continued. "So you know the bird they kept in the corner? Some fucking store mascot or something."

"The canary. I think it's called Kiiro," Aki said. He always brought it sunflower seeds.

"That's it. It kept on chirping during the whole thing. Louder and louder. Every time I raised my voice, it would squawk more. So I have to show the dipshit not to mess with the family. I reached into the cage, and the bird starts freaking out. Feathers everywhere, but I grabbed it and snapped its little neck."

Shoda joined in Fuse's laughter.

Even if the fishmonger didn't give them the Matsukawa discount, he was still a citizen. It was their duty to protect Kyoto's people. Shoda knew that, but still he laughed, and if Aki didn't join in, it would disrupt the harmony of the group. Aki couldn't call out his friends over some little bird.

"His mouth dropped open just like the fish in the display. I grabbed the order and walked out of there, and he didn't say a word. Watch it! The next time I go back there the piece of trash will probably piss himself."

They all laughed again.

"You want to hit the next bar with us, beautiful?" Fuse asked the woman that had joined them.

She winked. "If you'll be there, sugar, I'm game."

Maybe it was the bald head women found attractive about Fuse, or his confidence. Either way, Aki couldn't see it.

"Let's get out of here."

Shoda patted Aki on the back. "Since you got that promotion, you can get the next round of drinks."

Aki rubbed his neck. He didn't mind paying, but it was already past four. He usually tried to work out before Nao woke up at seven. If they headed back now, he could get a quick nap in before training.

"Are there even any bars open this late?" Aki asked.

Fuse laughed. "There's always a bar open."

After paying, the group strolled down the street in the darkness before daybreak. The September air clung heavily to Aki's skin. His long sleeves didn't help, but he couldn't wear anything else without getting looks of pity or disgust.

Shoda slung his arm around Aki's shoulder. "How about it, Hisona? One more drink? It might be the last time we can hang out."

Shoda's smile beckoned Aki to skip the gym. They had been buddies since high school, and if Aki was able to convince Nao to reduce the apprenticeship, Shoda and Fuse would leave headquarters in a few weeks. Fitting another outing in before he left would be impossible with three different schedules. Tonight would probably be their last night together.

"One more round, but that's it," Aki said.

They cheered, but all the bars in the area were closed. After a block, Fuse had gotten more preoccupied with both women.

"You know what, guys? I'm going to head off with these fine ladies and hit you up on that round of drinks next time," Fuse said.

Aki laughed. At least one of them would be with someone he liked.

Fuse disappeared, leaving Shoda and Aki behind.

Shoda squeezed Aki's arm. "Don't think you're getting out of buying me a beer that easily, Mr. Hot Shot Secretary."

"We got to find a place first."

"There should be one up another block."

The streets were quiet, except for trash workers, but they avoided even glancing toward Aki and Shoda. Even without the inward-facing arrows of the Matsukawa crest pinned on their shirts, they could never lose their yakuza swagger.

"I've been trying to suck up to the ward leader in the red-light district," Shoda said.

"You think the ward leader will move you there when your apprenticeship is over?"

"I think so, but who the fuck knows. I do everything they want, and I still feel like I haven't gotten anywhere."

"It hasn't gone unnoticed. There have been a few times Father Murata talked about how he wished all the recruits were as dedicated as you."

Shoda tugged on his ear. "I just gotta spend another six months cleaning toilets. Then probably another doing the same thing at one of the Kyoto wards. I joined the yakuza, not a maid service."

Aki laughed. "I felt that way, too. It takes time. People have to learn they can trust you before they hand over bigger duties."

"Is that so?"

"Wherever you go, I wish you the best. You'll make a name for yourself."

Even with the good wishes, Shoda's face remained tight. "It was easier for you."

The two passed through a narrow alley reeking of rotting fish and piss. The yellow trash bags took up so much space they had to walk single file.

"Maybe if I'd taken it up the ass, too, I would've gotten a cushy job answering phones by now," Shoda said.

"I don't just answ—"

"So you still have to suck his dick, too? Maybe we could both take turns. The fag might want some variety."

Aki's mouth slackened. "Shoda, you're drunk."

"And more clearheaded than ever before."

Shoda snatched a handful of Aki's chin-length hair and jerked him back. The world spun, and the first of the sun rays blinded Aki. Then Shoda's fist connected with the side of Aki's face, and he fell onto the stuffed trash bags.

"Shoda!" Aki cried out while all the hours of training he put in at the boxing gym fluttered away like a paper trapped in a whirlwind.

"B-but we're friends," Aki managed to say. "Why? Why are you doing this?"

Shoda grunted and drew his arm back again. "Huh? High school grad can't figure it out? You think you're better than the rest of us, don't you?"

Aki held up his arms, covering his face, but Shoda delivered a blow to his wrist that sent a shock wave of pain throughout Aki's body. But it didn't hurt as much as their breaking friendship.

"No! I never thought that," Aki pleaded.

"I'm going to fuck you up so bad Father Murata won't want to look at you. You two-toned freak!"

Another punch landed on Aki's stomach. The beer sloshing in his gut churned up his throat. His thoughts swirled as he slid down the trash bags and vomited. It splashed back onto his white hands.

Shoda kicked him in the ribs. A trail of acid followed the rest of the contents of Aki's stomach. Even with the copper taste of blood mixing with acid in his mouth, Aki knew the scuffle had to be a misunderstanding. They were best friends. Shoda just got a little hotheaded.

Aki wiped his mouth as Shoda stumbled back. Sure, Aki trained on a punching bag, but he never sparred with an actual person, let alone struck his best friend.

"Sho…"

Shoda reached into his pocket. Moonlight glistened off metal.

Aki scrambled to his feet. "Put the knife down!"

Shoda lunged forward, and Aki's quivering muscles grew hot. His nostrils flared, and he kicked Shoda in the shin. The blade flew to the ground. Aki scooped it up before Shoda could stagger to his feet.

Aki kept his grip on the knife. "Let's just go back to head-quarters and call it even."

Shoda groaned, then charged.

Aki's body tensed with the impact. They fell into the trash heap.

Shoda's hot breath licked at Aki's ear, and the knife Aki held became slick. Aki tried to pull it back, but it didn't budge.

"Hiso…" Shoda gurgled.

Aki slid out from under him, and the knife stayed put.

"You okay? Shoda!"

Blood smeared the plastic bags and covered Aki's hands. Aki sank to his knees and turned Shoda over. The knife stuck out of his gut like Mt. Fuji.

"Stay with me," Aki pleaded.

Shoda didn't move, and his eyes stared vacantly back at Aki. He gulped down a breath and pressed his bloody fingers against Shoda's neck. Aki couldn't feel anything but his own heart pounding in his ears.

Shoda was dead.

CHAPTER 02

THE RISING SUN revealed a blood pool around Shoda's body, like the Kamo River during rainy season.

Aki's chin trembled. "I didn't mean…"

There was so much blood.

A gasp that was not his drew Aki's gaze to the edge of the alleyway. A silhouetted figure rose out of nowhere, but as soon as Aki blinked, it disappeared. An unnatural frost climbed up his spine.

The figure must've been a death spirit taking Shoda's soul to the afterlife. No human could move so fast and leave such an unsettling feeling in his wake.

It was up to Aki to deal with Shoda's corpse and give him a proper Buddhist send-off into the afterlife, or at least as good as one got being cremated in the Matsukawa furnaces.

He needed to move Shoda before the trash collectors reached them.

The Matsukawa had never had a good relationship with the police. Even if Aki spoke the truth, Detective Yamada would pin whatever crime he wanted on him to make the Matsukawa look bad. Aki couldn't allow dishonor to fall on the family for a mistake he'd committed. He'd be excommunicated for killing the golden recruit.

Everything Aki had was because of Nao Murata. He was more than the godfather of the family; he was the moon on a dark night and the sun in the day. He accepted every blotched speck of skin and odd turn of phrase from Aki's thick Kyoto dialect when no one else had. Aki might as well change places with Shoda if it meant never being away from Nao.

"You have to do this," Aki said to himself.

He rubbed his bloodied hands on his black pants. He had disposed of many bodies during the Matsukawa war with the Korean mob. It only took a few hours to turn them into ash. He could do it to Shoda and hold a small funeral for him. Everything would be fine.

At least with the dark color of his shirt, the bloodstain wouldn't show. Aki rubbed his shirtsleeve to soak up what he could of the blood off the trash bags. He kneeled and rubbed his shirt against the pool, but it only smeared it more.

"There's so much."

His heart thrashed against his ribs. The sun was rising; everyone would see.

He had killed the Matsukawa golden boy.

No one would believe Shoda had attacked him first. Shoda and Aki were friends from way back. Aki remembered when he first saw Shoda. He'd driven his motorcycle right through a group of kids who were making fun of Aki about his skin. It had allowed Aki to run away unscathed, unlike the previous times.

Aki closed his eyes and pushed back the memories. It wasn't the time. He had to leave no evidence behind.

Dark smears streaked the sidewalk like a meteor shower. For the first time in as long as Aki could remember, his hands weren't white anymore.

Shoda's blood was everywhere.

Everyone would see.

Everyone would know he did it.

Aki clawed open one of the bags, and plastic bottles spilled out. From another bag, glass bottles tumbled to the ground. The trash workers would think an unwashed bottle had made the brown stain. It probably happened all the time. No one would want to stay long in an alley that stank of piss.

It would work.

It had to work.

Shoda was heavier than Aki would've thought, but he pulled Shoda's arm over his shoulder like a friend who'd had one too many. The scent of booze and vomit clung to their clothes, so anyone passing wouldn't get suspicious.

No one would look carefully enough to see the blade sticking out of Shoda's gut. He even wore black, too, so the blood didn't show. The only people up were garbage collectors anyway, and they knew their place.

Shoda grew heavier with each step down the quiet blocks. Aki pushed back his mourning and imagined Shoda as just another anonymous body to take care of.

The trash collectors were nowhere in sight when Aki propped the body against the car. He popped open the trunk, a tarp already lining it; the car did belong to the yakuza, after all. Aki hoisted Shoda into the trunk and slammed it shut.

Aki sighed and rubbed his shoulder as he got into the car. The sun glared in his eyes as he turned the key. No music played, but the clock's steady green display showed almost five thirty.

His jaw clenched, and he pressed his head against the steering wheel. Cremation took hours, and Nao would wake up before it finished. There would be no time to properly deal with the body and make it back to serve the godfather his morning tea.

The Matsukawa's punishments were worse than the police, and all of them would mean Aki's secretary position would be snuffed out. Aki pressed his lips together and tightened his grip on the wheel. He'd make Shoda look like he'd run away from the family, and then Aki wouldn't have to worry about confessing.

He had to pretend nothing had happened. He would go to the gym like he always did, then fulfill his duty to Nao. Once night fell and he was dismissed, he'd deal with the body.

CHAPTER 03

"YOU FORGOT the condom," Kohta said.

Aki's eyes narrowed.

"It's all over your face how much you want Nao to bang you again. He's been too busy to notice, so put a condom next to his tea, and he'll know."

"How dare you be so crass talking about Father Murata."

"You don't have to hide it from me. I might be new, but even I heard all about you and Nao banging all hours of the night."

Aki clenched his teeth, pain swelling from the tightness of his jaw. Nao had allowed Kohta to call him by his first name, or simply boss, when all the other recruits wouldn't dare use anything but the proper title of Father Murata. Sure, Aki thought of Father Murata as Nao, but Aki wouldn't cross the line and say it out loud. Kohta had no respect for family traditions.

"Boss could probably use the break, and you've been tense since you got back from the gym this morning. I know Nao's impressive, so he'll be able to fix you right up." Kohta winked.

The walls of the kitchen closed in each time Kohta spouted nonsense. He was a total moron, and Aki had no idea why Nao allowed Kohta to take on the Matsukawa apprenticeship.

Aki tapped his finger on the counter and caught sight of the butsudan, the family altar with the photos of past Matsukawa godfathers and a few personal ones Nao kept there.

No. Aki knew exactly why Kohta had been allowed to join.

Kohta's wavy blond hair resembled the man Nao had wanted to spend the rest of his life with. If Aki squinted, Kohta would be the walking embodiment of Nao's dead lover. Aki could never compete with him for Nao's affection. Not when Aki's heart-shaped face, Korean heritage, and dark hair stood at odds with everything Nao desired.

"Go finish your chores!" Aki snapped. "You don't earn your keep by getting fucked anymore."

Kohta shrugged. "Usually Shoda gives me a list of items, but I haven't seen him today."

"Then get a rag and start scrubbing."

Aki turned his back and pulled down a tin from Nao's impressive tea cabinet. The balled oolong leaves resembled Shoda's crumpled corpse. Even when Aki had showered at the gym, he couldn't forget with the blood-soaked water flowing off his body and down the drain. Aki had gotten lucky since no one ever wanted to shower close to him.

Aki could not clutter his thoughts with personal issues. All aspects of his life belonged to Nao Murata until he deemed the working day finished. Until then, Shoda would have to wait. Aki closed the tea tin lid, and the image of Shoda disappeared.

Nao didn't have any major meetings today, so a dark astringent tea wouldn't match Nao's reluctance toward them. He needed something lighter to match the festival he'd planned on attending. Aki grabbed another tin and opened the lid. The dark leaves were as black as a sealed furnace and rolled into long fingerlike twigs. The smell of damp earth like a light rain in a plum orchid would intensify once the leaves steeped. It was a tea worthy of the day, and of Nao.

"Didn't Shoda go drinking with you last night?" Kohta asked, still hovering in the kitchen like an idiot.

"We split up. I headed to the gym, and he wanted to hit another bar."

Aki prepared the rest of the tea, water set at the perfect temperature and the right amount of leaves for the pot in the mesh infuser basket. Everything was in order except for Kohta.

"I guess that means I have the day off," he said.

Aki crossed his arms. "Of course not. I told you to grab a rag and scrub, which you haven't even started. Then you have to do your usual duties, as well as Shoda's until he comes back. And when he does, I'll let him decide what punishment your insubordination deserves."

Aki crossed his arms and waited until Kohta took out a rag and scrubbed the counters. At least he knew better than to open his mouth and say something idiotic again. Aki shook his head. He'd try to convince Nao to make the apprenticeship six months so Kohta could leave that much sooner. He couldn't even wear the jumpsuit of an apprentice correctly, choosing to adorn it with an expensive Louis Vuitton belt. The large LV buckle looked stupid on top of being impractical.

"So when you take off, who works as Nao's secretary?" Kohta asked.

"I don't take off. My duty is to Father Murata."

"But you had yesterday off."

"I was still on call."

"Don't you think that's a little much, never having a day off? Maybe if you put in a word with Nao, we could share the job."

"Don't be silly. You're not even considered a real Matsukawa until you formally drink sake with Murata at the ceremony." Aki laughed and grabbed the tea tray.

"But you deserve to have a few days off a week. You have to answer his phone and make tea."

"There's more to it than that."

Kohta grinned. "Come on, I know he doesn't fuck you half as much as the others say. If he did, you wouldn't get that mad look on your face when I talk about him. I told you I only sucked him off once, but then he realized I was straight and told me to stop."

Every muscle inside Aki quivered. "Get back to work."

Carrying the tea tray up the stairs came as a welcome duty for Aki. He knocked on Nao's office door and waited for the godfather's acknowledgement before entering.

Aki gave a low formal bow while Nao nodded and mumbled a good morning. Nobu, a black hairless cat, raced inside before Aki could shut the door. At twenty-six, Nao was the youngest godfather in Japan, and at twenty, it put Aki as the youngest with the honorable job as secretary.

A smile grew on Nao's face at the cat. She received a warmer welcome than Aki had gotten. Still, Aki drew in a breath and reminded himself of the formality of his and Nao's shared morning ritual.

Nao's office could sit up to ten people. Dark leather sofas and chairs surrounded a coffee table on three sides. Nao's wooden desk stood at the head with the Japanese flag hanging on the wall behind him, along with the Matsukawa crest. When Aki had first joined the yakuza less than six months ago, he never thought he'd be coming in and out of the godfather's room so often.

Aki placed the tray on the coffee table. The round teapot and burnt-orange and yellow rimless cups were ideal for the summer months.

Nao's long fingers turned the tea leaves trapped within their wire basket infuser, and all Aki wanted to do was gaze into Nao's chestnut-colored eyes. His skin appeared paler than normal against his harsh black suit, but Aki's hands were an off-putting paper-white against his.

"The plum oolong?" Nao asked.

"Father Murata, your knowledge of tea is without comparison."

The corners of Nao's mouth perked up. Aki always pushed his Kyoto dialect around Nao to an almost comical inflection. But each little half smile Nao gave urged Aki a little more. Perhaps one day his accent would stroke some nerve within Nao, and they'd finally act on the rumors about them.

Nao cleared his throat and stroked the cat, who curled up on his lap. "What's the schedule for today?"

"Your usual morning schedule for the gym, then the Seiryu-e Dragon festival at the Kiyomizu Temple this afternoon."

Nao nodded, and with Nobu's loud purring, they waited for the tea to steep. When it was done, Aki grasped the handle and lifted to pour Nao's tea. Pain shot through his wrist, and he grabbed the handle with both hands. He bit his lip and poured the scented tea. The gangly use of both hands was unsightly. Nao deserved better.

"What happened?" Nao raised an eyebrow.

Acid burned in Aki's stomach. He couldn't cover up the pain with makeup like he could for the bruises. "I went to the gym this morning and hurt my wrist. I'm sorry for my inconvenience and inadequacy."

Nao said nothing and picked up the tea. The distance between them during the exchange ached in Aki's heart. When Nao had been in the delirium of an infection, he'd touched Aki's hand while he reached for a glass. The brief contact had driven Aki drunk with desire all day, but since Nao's wound had closed, a chasm had grown between them.

Nao nodded after sipping the tea, a small signal Aki had made the tea correctly. Of course he had. He wouldn't serve anything subpar to Nao.

"The unwrapped leaves create a beautiful contrast to how they looked before," Nao said between sips.

A few more sips, and Aki poured his own cup. If Aki couldn't touch Nao's skin again, at least Nao allowed him to drink from the same pot.

"Don't be so hard on Kohta," Nao said. "You make this pissed-off look whenever he enters a room."

Aki tugged at his tie but nodded.

"We don't have as many recruits as we used to. So don't drive the new ones away."

"I will happily do whatever you desire," Aki said. "Perhaps given that the recruits don't have a clear estimate of how long the apprenticeship lasts, it may deter people from joining."

It would also give Aki a clear idea of when to expect Kohta out of headquarters.

"I guess switching back to six months would make everyone happier. I just hate the idea of shrinking it from a year like it used to be when I joined." Nao slouched a little in his chair and scratched behind the cat's ear. "What do you think?"

The cat meowed in response and rubbed against Nao's hand. Even the cat's opinion was more valued.

Nao glanced up. "I'll get you when I'm ready to leave, Aki."

Aki's knees weakened every time Nao said his first name. Yet using his first name was the only intimacy Nao wanted.

Aki bowed before exiting the room. His small end table of a desk stood in a nook between the landing of the stairs and the hallway to the other rooms. The space made it easier for Nao to get Aki, but in reality, it was because Nao was the biggest technophobe Aki had ever seen. Even the landline phone had been banished from the office to live underneath Aki's end table.

He plopped in his chair and took a sip of tea. Even if he had deemed Aki the only person in the family worthy of making his tea, Aki was nowhere near as obsessed. Maybe he and Nao were too different. Maybe it wasn't even worth fantasizing about more shared kisses between them.

Fuse walked over, rubbing his bald head. "Have you seen Shoda?"

Aki swallowed. "He hasn't come back yet?"

"I never heard him get back."

"I don't know, then."

"Did he meet someone at the bar?" Fuse asked. "Was she hot, or was he too wasted to realize he went home with a pig?"

All the muscles in Aki's body tensed. No one had ever been so concerned about Shoda for as long as Aki had been in the Matsukawa, and the one day he's gone, everyone wanted to know where he was.

"He was talking to some woman when I left to go to the gym. Probably sleeping off a hangover with her."

"You've been up this whole time?"

Aki doubted he could go to sleep even if he tried.

"Can't piss off Murata by falling asleep on the job. With enough energy drinks, I'll make it until tonight."

"Maybe you try and text him. If word gets out he's missing, he can kiss his golden-boy status with Murata goodbye."

Aki laughed. "That's for sure. When I see him, I'll tell him you're looking for him."

Fuse rubbed the back of his neck. "Thanks. I'm just worried. It's not like him."

He walked down the stairs, leaving Aki alone. Nao's coo came muffled through the door as he played with his cat.

Thick saliva coated Aki's throat, and when he tried to swallow, he hiccupped for breath.

He'd killed his best friend.

Then dumped his bloodied body in the trunk.

They'd all find out the horrors he'd committed.

He'd be shunned out of the family, and then... then he'd have nothing.

Aki wrapped his arms around himself. The beating of his heart echoed in his ears. His hands trembled as it shook him to his core.

His fingers grazed over the Matsukawa crest pinned to the lapel on the suit Nao had given him. Aki still had a family. He still belonged somewhere. Aki gulped, pushing away the thick coating along his throat.

He opened the small nightstand drawer big enough to hold a stack of multicolored origami paper. He had paper tucked away everywhere Nao went. It wasn't like the head of the mob needed letters typed up, so Aki's secretary position was reduced to following Nao around and answering his phone, which left him with plenty of free time.

Aki grabbed a small stack of paper and placed it next to the half-empty teacup. His shaking hands slowed with each fold of a crimson page. He scraped the edge of the crease with his nail, and by the time he reversed the valley folds into mountain folds, his hands grew steady.

Shoda was nothing but a body like the others Aki had burned in the mountains surrounding Kyoto.

It wasn't his fault Shoda died. He attacked Aki. Everyone would agree Aki had every right to defend himself. If anything, Shoda had caused the whole predicament. Aki shouldn't feel guilty over someone else's actions. Aki should be pissed Shoda made such trouble for him.

Aki opened the finished crane as Nao emerged from his office.

"It's the first time I've seen you mess up. Is something distracting you?" Nao asked.

Aki blinked at the lopsided crane and frowned.

"Everything is all right, Father Murata." Aki crumpled up the crane.

"What do you do with all those cranes, anyway?"

"I give them away."

"Like on benches in parks?"

Aki smiled. At least Nao faked interest in something he worked on for once.

"There's a website online. People get together and make thousand-crane chains for the sick. I usually make a hundred chain and send them away to the event organizer every week."

"Who's getting the ones you're making now?"

"I don't know yet."

Nao picked up the crane. "Maybe that's why you messed up. You didn't have a clear idea who the crane was for. Time to pull the car around."

"Whatever you desire."

Nao frowned, but the glint in his eyes wasn't one of anger. He walked away. His ass always looked so damn good in those pinstriped tailored pants. He always taunted Aki in them and even wore blazers that framed his butt perfectly.

Aki took one last sip of his tea before strolling to the carport around the back of the main house. He jingled the keys in his pocket and breathed in the fresh summer air.

Aki walked around the car like he always did to scrub off any dust ruining the shiny onyx finish to the luxury Japanese model. He paused at the back bumper and cleaned off a dirty spot with his handkerchief. But when he pulled the cloth away, it was stained red.

His mouth drew into a thin line as he squirmed to wipe the rest of the bumper clean. He thought he'd washed everything off after he'd shoved the body in there. The tarp inside must have had a hole in it for the blood to leak. He needed to rearrange Shoda so more blood wouldn't leak out while driving Nao around.

Aki popped open the trunk.

His eyes grew wide.

Shoda was gone.

CHAPTER 04

AKI'S HAND trembled.

He covered his mouth and stepped away from the empty trunk. Even the tarp had disappeared.

Shoda might've been alive the whole time and opened the trunk himself. Then Aki wouldn't have to deal with his body, only the awkward conversation between them. Hopefully there would be no hard feelings considering Shoda had attacked him first.

Aki shook his head.

No.

Shoda had died.

He'd shown no signs of life while Aki dragged him through the streets, and he wouldn't suddenly come to life after being locked in a trunk for four hours.

Sweat greased Aki's palms. Someone must've taken the body.

"What's taking so long?"

Aki jumped at Nao's words, then bowed. "I'm sorry for my transgression."

Nao stepped closer, and all of Aki's muscles tensed as Nao examined the trunk. Aki held his breath. Aki couldn't see any sign a body had been inside, but Nao could unravel people with a single gaze like a chef skinning a fish. Aki wouldn't put it past Nao somehow being able to sense everything that had ever happened in the trunk.

"What were you doing?" Nao asked.

"There was some dust I wanted to clean off." Aki bit his lip and shut the trunk.

"Then have one of the new recruits wash it later. As my secretary, stuff like that is beneath you now."

"Anything you desire."

Nao's all-knowing gaze looked through Aki and saw everything. Nao took his breath away, but Aki couldn't look away, too trapped within his infatuation for the other man.

Nao cocked his head and lowered his voice. "Are you sure nothing's wrong? You can tell me."

It was impossible to tell him what happened.

Despite training, Aki couldn't disarm Shoda without killing him. With so few recruits joining and the large casualties sustained by the family during the turf war a few months back, Nao's dissatisfaction would be too much for Aki to bear.

"I had some trouble sleeping," Aki squeaked out.

"It must be difficult being a light sleeper with so many people living at headquarters."

Aki's heart thumped. He'd mentioned being a light sleeper in passing. He'd never thought Nao would care to remember something so trivial.

"I'm humbled by your concern, but I manage."

"Maybe you should buy earplugs," Nao said.

"I like to be aware of what's going on around me."

"But you don't have to do that now. You just need to hear the phone ring, not every creak the house makes when someone walks by. You get paid enough to afford your own place."

Aki's lips thinned into a line. "That is correct."

"See? Then you wouldn't have to share a room with the recruits. You need your sleep."

Bile churned up Aki's throat. He swallowed it back down, but Nao's words stung worse than the acid.

Aki woke most nights to the soft groans of Nao trapped within the midst of a nightmare. Aki had always been the one to bring him out of the horrors. Aki clung on to the precious moments alone with Nao. For only in the dead of night between the lucidity and the delirium of dreams did Nao's façade fall.

Was suggesting he move out Nao's subtle way of telling him to stop waking him? Aki rubbed his eyes. Perhaps if he traded his contacts for glasses, Nao would like him more. He had said Aki looked cute in them once… then lost consciousness because of the infection.

The only hope Aki could cling to was to deal quietly with Shoda's body, wherever it was, and continue his loyal dedication to Nao. Given enough time, Nao would see how much Aki loved him.

"What do you think?" Nao asked.

"It's an interesting proposition, Father Murata."

"Then take some time to consider it."

Aki bowed his head, hoping his hair covered his eyes. "Allow me to take care of the bag for you."

All Aki could do was serve Nao in small ways like carrying his bag and opening the car door. Even then Aki screwed over the family. Each second Aki didn't confess would make his punishment that much harsher when what happened came to light.

Yet, it was wrong to think about himself while working. His life was a speck when compared to the family and Nao.

Aki took in a deep breath as Nao slid into the back seat without a word. Aki placed the bag in the passenger seat and drove out of headquarters.

"What would happen if you were called at night?" Aki asked.

"Huh?"

Aki's fingers turned whiter as they clutched the steering wheel. "If I move out, and your phone rings, who would answer? If you needed to leave, who'd drive you there?"

"Someone else in the house."

Nao could've shot him and the bullet would've hurt less. It wouldn't even be a specific person. Anyone could fulfill his official duties.

"You're still the only person I really trust." Nao rubbed his neck. "So you'd still have my cell phone to answer calls. Then if it was important enough, you'd call headquarters and someone would wake me to talk with you. If it was important enough that I needed to go somewhere, then I would have to wait for you come."

"Then it would have to be somewhere close by."

"Who is it that you share a room with now?"

"Fuse and Shoda."

Nao sighed. "It might be time to graduate those two and double up the other rooms when we get new recruits."

"I wouldn't want to cause any extra burden to the family."

Aki caught Nao's gaze through the rearview mirror. Nao's brow wrinkled.

"Shoda I don't mind moving up soon, but Fuse?" Nao shook his head. "He's still a bastard, but we need everyone we can get to fill positions. Maybe I can stick him in the ward with the heavy Korean populations. Then, when they attack again, he could get his aggression out there, instead of insulting the snack food I offer him."

"When?"

"Their leader is a psycho. It's not a matter of if the Korean mob strikes again, but when. Shoda might be good in that ward, too. Given enough time, he might even become the ward leader."

It took all of Aki's strength not to change the pitch in his voice. "Shoda's talents would be useful there. A wise choice."

Nao nodded and stared out the window. His silence drove Aki's thoughts to more sinister events.

Everywhere Aki looked became drenched by Shoda's blood. The dark patches of sidewalk unfolded images of the fight. Maybe he could stop by a shrine after dealing with Shoda's body to ward off any lingering evil. Still, how could someone he saw as a brother want to hurt him for getting a promotion? They'd scrubbed the same floors, slept in the same room, rode motorcycles throughout high school together.

Maybe Shoda's hatred lingered after his death and fueled his corpse? Aki slid his hands down the wheel. It wasn't some supernatural awakening that moved the body. One of the newest recruits probably saw the blood and moved him. If Aki was lucky, one of them had already handled the disposal. Aki just needed to find out which one did it.

◆ • ◆

Aki parked outside the yakuza boxing gym and opened Nao's door. A group of skipping high schoolers gathered outside. Eventually they'd become Matsukawa. Aki had been one of them years back.

Nao dug in his pocket and pulled out a thousand-yen note. He'd been working on one of the older teens for a while.

"Go get me the newspapers." Nao handed the money to the teen.

He scurried off, and Nao and Aki stepped inside.

While the exterior of the gym was little more than gray concrete, the interior blossomed with colors from the tattoos brandished by more than half the men there. Everything from dragons slithering down backs to gardens of cherry blossoms were on display. Most of the newer members only had the in-ward-facing arrows of the Matsukawa crest on their arm or over their hearts since full-body tattoos were falling out of fashion.

Nao's arrival halted everyone mid-workout. They all bowed formally and greeted Nao with a hearty good morning. A smiled spread across Nao's face, and he replied and wished everyone a good workout.

Usually, the daily trips to the gym left Aki's body tingling. When Nao sparred, he'd take off his shirt to show off the red phoenix tattooed on his back. Aki would steal glances at the lean muscles Nao kept hidden under his suits. Nao could go from cool and collected to snapping someone's neck if he sensed betrayal. Being so close to such a powerful man while he fought ignited every lust-filled fantasy Aki had acquired in his twenty years of life.

Bunta, the gym manager, strolled over. A dragon tattoo ran down one side of his chest, and koi fish swam up the other.

"Any volunteers today?" Nao asked.

Bunt scratched at his graying goatee. "I managed to convince someone."

"Good. I'll be ready in a half hour."

After winning the battle against his infection, Nao had out-skilled every Matsukawa in the ring.

"You feeling all right?" Bunta asked Aki.

Nao stopped and turned back. His intense gaze bore into Aki.

"What happened?" he asked.

Bunta answered, "It was his first time in the ring, and he got banged up even with all the protective gear on."

The fight had concealed any injuries from Shoda's attack. Aki bit his lip.

"That's why you couldn't hold the teapot correctly."

Aki's chin lowered. "I humbly—"

"Be careful next time."

Nao shook his head and headed to the changing rooms. Aki let out a long breath.

"You'll do better with more practice," Bunta said.

Aki walked off to find his usual seat in the glass-walled offices along the back. One of the metal desk drawers squeaked as he grabbed a stack of origami paper left there. Aki sighed and began to fold while stealing glances at the phoenix dancing on Nao's back.

A crane emerged out of the paper within seconds, and Aki grabbed the next sheet. Each crane concealed the folds used in their creation like a secret only Aki knew. There had to be a way Aki could figure out the secret of what happened to Shoda's body.

Ten minutes later, cranes covered the desk, and a high schooler brought the newspapers. Aki let him keep the change.

Aki's stomach twisted like it was folding its own origami creation as he scanned through the headlines for any mention of an assault or bloody trash bags.

Nao's phone rang in Aki's pocket. He groaned.

"This is Hisona," Aki answered and continued to flip through the pages.

"What took you so long?" Kurosawa asked.

Kurosawa was the Matsukawa's underboss and acted as the middleman between the street and legal branches. He allowed information to be passed from one side to another without either losing face and acted as an extra layer of separation between Nao and the mob's activities.

"Sorry," Aki mumbled.

"There was a fight near our bars downtown last night."

The page dropped out of Aki's hand.

Everyone knew.

He held his breath and fought to keep his voice steady. "Oh?"

"Our patrol found it this morning before the garbage crew came. They'd ripped open the trash in an attempt to hide it."

Aki muscles tensed. "Was it a bar fight or something?"

He couldn't believe he was withholding information. No one who lied to anyone in the family could be trusted.

"Too much blood for a simple fight," Kurosawa said. "The ward leader wants to make sure it wasn't the Korean mob trying to cause trouble again. So he's going to interview everyone in the area."

Aki crumpled the edge of the newspaper. "Are the police involved as well?"

"You know how they are. No body, no crime."

He couldn't properly search headquarters for Shoda's body until Nao dismissed him, but he wouldn't be safe until Shoda's body was ash.

"I'll call back once we get more info. It's still too early in the day to interview the night crowd."

Aki gulped. "So, everyone's thinking it's the Koreans?"

"Don't say Korean in front of Father Murata, or he'll flip. You know how he is. If a Korean stepped foot in Kyoto, it meant a Matsukaswa fucked up by not keeping the border tight. So be cautious. Say there was a fight and that we're looking into it."

"Without fail."

Kurosawa hung up.

Aki's pulse pounded in his ears. He couldn't tell Nao about the fight. He didn't need to know anyway since it wasn't the Koreans.

Aki slipped the phone into his pocket and folded another crane. Shoda had to be somewhere. Aki mentally retraced his steps. After stuffing him in the trunk, he'd headed to the gym and then to headquarters to prepare Nao's tea.

Aki shot up.

The security cameras at the gym. Whatever happened to Shoda's body would show up in the footage.

In a few quick strides, Aki opened the door to the security office. A man munched away on chips while staring at the four TV screens.

"Father Murata wanted me to look at something," Aki said.

"What is it?" He cleaned his hands on his pants, crumbs and grease staining the fabric. "I can pull it up on the big screen."

"I need to work on this alone." Aki rolled his eyes. "You understand how Murata is."

"You don't have to tell me twice. I'll be outside if you need any help."

The door shut, and Aki brought up the footage. He sped up the video, watching the different angles of the car during his first trip to the gym.

Nothing happened.

The car sat undisturbed for several minutes. Then someone approached. Aki paused the image and stared at the man. Aki didn't know his name, but he greeted them every time they visited the ward leader where the bar fight happened.

The guy must've been on patrol when the fight broke out. They had only gone to yakuza-friendly bars, so anyone in the family would've recognized Aki. His shoulders tightened, and his eyes shut.

Someone knew what he had done and followed him to the gym. They must've taken Shoda's body as proof of Aki's treachery against the family.

Aki's hand jerked as he played the event in real time. The man approached the car, then walked around it before stopping at the trunk. Aki held his breath as the man put his hand on the car.

The door to the office opened, and Aki jumped.

"Why are you in here?" Nao demanded.

Aki blinked at Nao's reflection on the video screen. The man on the screen was stuck in a permanent pause with his hand on the trunk's lock.

Aki was going to die. There was no other punishment for what he did.

CHAPTER 05

"WHY ARE YOU looking at security footage?" Nao asked.

"I thought I saw something suspicious."

Aki's insides thrashed like paper fed through a shredder. He'd lied to Nao. Not a tiny lie wrapped around a hint of truth, but a bold-faced you-can-suck-it lie. Aki rubbed his thumb along the jagged white splotches on his palm, then stared at the polished shoes Nao had bought for him. Nao had given him everything, and he betrayed him.

"Was it the Koreans?" Nao asked.

"I haven't found…"

Nao's approach took Aki's breath away. The godfather's skin glistened with a light sheen of sweat, and his raven-black hair was plastered to his neck. An intense power that would bring any man to his knees radiated off him.

"Let's watch it, then." Nao leaned over and started the footage.

The man ran his hand over the trunk.

"Who is that?" Nao asked.

"I-I'm not sure."

"Why is he by the car?"

But then the man walked away without even opening the trunk. Blood could've dripped out, and he decided to report it back to his superior. Or he might've realized who the car belonged to and knew better than to open his mouth.

"This footage is from long before we arrived," Nao said.

"When I cleaned the dirt on the car, there was a small scratch, too."

Aki swallowed. Lies weren't supposed to come out so easily.

Nao crossed his arms. "I wouldn't put it past those Korean bastards to do something cowardly and scratch my car."

They watched the sped-up video play as Aki gnawed on his lower lip. If someone else had noticed the blood and broken into the trunk… There wouldn't be enough lies Aki could tell to keep Nao's trust.

Nao couldn't take his gaze off the screen.

People walked by the car, but no one else touched it.

"Maybe there was a scratch from before and that guy tried to clean it off," Nao said.

"You're right. I'm probably imagining things."

"We'll get someone to interview him. Concealing mistakes is not something we allow in the family."

Aki was screwed until he'd burned all evidence of Shoda's existence.

"Come out," Nao said. "I want to watch you practice with Hiro."

They left the room and entered the gym. Aki glanced at Hiro's toned arms and gulped. Hiro was the best fighter the Matsukawa had. If it wasn't for the crest tattooed on his chest, he'd be competing in the major leagues.

"Forgive me, I don't have any clothes with me," Aki said.

Nao crossed his arms. "You're dressed in a suit most of the time. It's important to know how to fight in one."

Escaping Nao's plan was futile. If he wanted to see Aki's street-fighting skills in action, nothing would stop it from happening.

Hiro warmed up and jabbed a few punches in the air while Aki gnawed on his lip. Nao didn't have to push him. The hardest skill Aki's job required was keeping Nao's phone charged and driving the speed limit.

"Let's get this show going," Nao said.

Aki slipped off his jacket.

"See!" Nao yelled. "He could've gotten a punch in right there."

"Forgive me. I didn't know we'd started."

"That's exactly my point." Nao glanced to Hiro. "Pretend it's for real. Aki needs to learn how important training is."

Hiro nodded. "Of course, Father Murata."

He lunged forward, and before Aki could blink, Hiro's fist slammed into his stomach. Aki gasped, the blow knocking the wind out of him. He scurried to stand, but Hiro kicked him in the gut and sent Aki to his knees.

Somewhere among the pain and the light-headedness, Hiro's face merged with Shoda's.

"Keep your eyes open," Nao called.

His voice hovered over Aki like a god speaking down to him, but all of Shoda's movements blurred as Aki's world splintered in pain from each new blow.

"Watch and anticipate where he's going to be," the god spoke again.

Agony burned over Aki's throbbing ribs like a river of tea, while the discarded leaves punctured his skin. Shoda loomed over him. Aki hadn't meant to hurt him.

The knife, the pain—it wasn't supposed to be a night of death, but a night to celebrate in friendship.

"I didn't mean—Shoda, please… Stop."

Aki's head thumped against the mat, and his vision blurred. Shoda was going to take him away to the land of the dead to join him.

Through the darkness Nao emerged, kneeling beside him. Aki blinked and smiled, the taste of copper lingering in his mouth.

"You there?" Nao asked.

Aki rubbed his eyes, careful not to smudge the concealer covering up the bruises.

"How often do you go to the gym?" Nao asked.

"Three times a week."

"Double that until you can hold your own."

Nao stepped back, and Hiro offered his hand to help Aki stand. He closed his eyes; if only Nao would touch him again. The little spark of contact could fuel Aki for months, but Nao had already disappeared into the showers.

"What time do you come? I can show you some moves," Hiro said.

He was only trying to get on Nao's good side by offering help. Aki shook his head and swallowed down the blood pooling in his mouth. He didn't need to be humiliated more.

◆ ● ◆

Aki always enjoyed his breakfast with Nao, but the traditional miso soup, rice, and grilled fish had taken Aki a bit more time to get used to. He and Nao would sit in the same corner booth. Nao would silently read the newspaper until an article would remind him of a story, and he'd start talking.

Some tales were of him as a teenager within the yakuza, and others would be during his short-lived retirement as a tea merchant. Either way, between the soup and pickled vegetables, Aki could pretend they were lovers.

Aki nodded along to Nao's story. The wings of cranes he folded turned into knives. His hand dripped with blood once more. Aki steadied his breath and rubbed the illusion out of his eyes.

"You okay?" Nao asked for the second time.

He didn't have to pretend like he really cared.

"Didn't sleep well," Aki mumbled.

At least that wasn't a lie. The coffee he drank could only chase away his drowsiness for so long. They enjoyed their leisurely breakfast turned lunch until it was time to go to the festival.

When it came time, they left the restaurant, and Aki drove to the mountains surrounding Kyoto.

The two men hiked up the stone stairway to the Kiyomizu Temple concealed along a heavy tree line. In the humid summer, Aki's suit clung to him like the blood that had soaked through his shirt. Aki rubbed his forehead and yawned. He had to stay in the moment. He couldn't worry about his problems while on duty.

Nao stepped to the edge of the wide stairway and stared at the vista while people walked around them.

"Kyoto is the most beautiful city in the world," Nao said. "Isn't this view wonderful?"

Aki had spent most of his time trying to put one foot in front of the other on the steep incline, instead of taking in the scenery.

The red wood and stone-blue tile roof of the Kiyomizu Temple jutted out over the trees. Between ascending stairs and small vignettes to trees, other minor deities were honored. The view was pretty, but perhaps it was Aki's Korean side that couldn't allow him to stare into it with the same undying awe.

Yet the gentle rushing of the waterfall blocked out the noise from the crowd. For a single moment, it was just him and Nao on the path.

"It's pretty," Aki said.

"That's why we protect Kyoto. So its people can enjoy its wonders."

A black-and-white cat weaved in and out between the people before poking its head into a shrub and pouncing on a bug.

Drumming echoed down the mountainside, followed by the chanting of monks. It broke Nao out of the spell the scenery cast.

"Let's not miss it," Nao said.

It didn't matter how late they came, because once people caught sight of their lapel pins, they parted ways. No one wanted to associate with a yakuza, and before the dragon emerged for the ceremony, Nao and Aki had a prime view of the temple's main veranda.

Monks dressed in period warrior costumes carried down the green dragon. Its gilded scales shimmered as it snaked down the stairs and through the gate to the veranda. They danced in a circle, carrying the crafted dragon on sticks while a line of monks rang bells and chanted behind it. Twice a year the dragon god Seiryu drank from the waterfall at the temple then returned to its watch over Kyoto.

The whole thing took less than twenty minutes before the monks escorted the dragon to snake its way to another part of the temple and surrounding township. Nao lit up like the dragon was real and he hadn't seen the festival every year of his life. His eyes glistened with a new sheen, and his smile grew wider than Aki had ever seen.

People shuffled out once the ceremony was over, going to the other shrines along the mountain or lingering around the hall of the temple.

"Legend has it if you jump off the Kiyomizu Temple and live, your wish will come true." Nao stared out over the veranda.

There was at least a fifty-meter drop, before hitting the tree line clinging to the steep hill. After that was the steep, rocky hill. It looked impossible to survive.

Nao laughed. "I think your one thousand cranes are an easier way to get a wish."

"What would you wish for, Father Murata?"

Aki rubbed his hand with his thumb. It wasn't his place to ask, but it came rushing out without him thinking.

The far-off gaze returned to Nao's eyes. "Would it be unfair to call someone up from the dead?" Nao asked.

"I don't think so."

Pain swelled in Aki's heart. If he had one wish, it would be for Shoda to be alive. Even if he betrayed their friendship in his final moments, there were still years of memories shared between them.

Nao stepped away. "It's illegal now anyway."

Aki's pulse thudded in his ears as they prayed, then strolled back down the stairs. Aki's limbs grew heavy as he fought to stay awake with each one.

"There's that cat again," Nao said. "You think Nobu would like a playmate?"

"Nobu's still a kitten. Her energy would probably wear the street cat out."

Nao squatted and clicked his tongue. The cat peeked at him through the shrubs. Her black nose was adorable.

"Come on, kitty," Nao cooed.

The cat emerged from the bushes with something in its mouth. Aki's eyes narrowed. The shape wasn't right to be a bird. The cat trotted through the people and dropped its trophy on Aki's shoe.

A woman beside him screamed.

CHAPTER 06

THE CAT'S EARS drew back at the woman's screams. It scurried off, leaving its trophy on Aki's shoe. The breath caught in his throat. The cat had dropped a severed hand right on his shoe.

Aki kicked it off, but it merely flopped over, landing palm side up. The cut on the wrist was clean, as if a saw had sliced through the bone. No blotches of decomposition had formed, so it was either a fresh kill or had been frozen. The Matsukawa had never given Aki a chilled body to dispose of, so he couldn't tell if there were signs of frost.

"Fuck," Nao said.

The panic spread. More people screamed and fumbled down the stairs. A few people called the police, but hysteria slurred their words. Even with chaos around him, Nao remained calm.

"We have to stay close or else Detective Yamada will find some excuse to go knocking at headquarters' door and demand I speak with him."

Aki pulled at his jacket cuff. "Whatever you desire."

"The lazy bastard would probably plant some evidence on my desk and arrest me so he wouldn't have to do any real police work."

Nao strolled off while security blocked off the area. Aki followed him through a new set of torii gates and into one of the minor shrines.

They passed a statue of a rabbit and a building selling charms. A layer of lanterns hung underneath the blue tiled roof. Nao stooped beside a large rock. A thick rope lay over the stone with another similar stone meters away.

"It's usually so crowded here. Maybe we should count ourselves lucky," Nao said.

"Will the detective know to look for us here?"

Nao laughed. "A cat put a hand on your shoe. Someone's keeping an eye on the yakuza who wander off."

A light breeze shook the lanterns and rattled the white wooden strips that covered the side. Each one had a couple's names. Aki looked for some kind of plaque detailing why they were bestowed the honor but found none.

"Why are there only names of couples?" Aki asked.

"Haven't you been here before? They found the love they prayed for and returned to offer their thanks."

"Forgive me. I haven't traveled to as many historic sites. I'm learning more each time we venture out."

"Then you don't know if you'll ever find love."

The wistful look in Nao's eyes made Aki's heart flutter. Of course he had found love. He loved Nao, and no one else would ever do.

Nao pointed to the rock beside him. "You have to walk to the other love rock with your eyes closed. If you make it, you'll find love."

The rocks looked farther from each other than before.

"Go ahead and give it a shot. I made it, and a few days later, I met Shinya."

If Nao could find the love of his life after walking to a rock, perhaps when Aki completed it, the god of love would guide Nao's heart to him.

Aki stood before one of the rocks. The other sat directly ahead.

"I'm ready," Aki said.

"Make sure to keep your eyes closed. If you open them before you get to the rock, then it won't happen."

Aki covered his eyes with his hands and took a step forward. If he took small steps he could stay on a straight course. The wind picked up, and the musk of incense drifted in the humid air. He swallowed and continued to take his hesitant sojourn.

"Want me to guide you?" Nao asked.

"Are you allowed to do it?"

"It just means you'll have someone help you find your love."

If Nao helped, it could bind them together.

"Am I far off?" Aki asked.

"Take two steps right."

Aki followed the directions, trying to concentrate on his steps and not the people talking in the distance. They must've been the police. They'd be at the shrine soon wanting to interview them.

Aki bit his lip. No. He needed to focus on Nao so the shrine god knew exactly who Aki wanted to find love with. Perhaps it was asking a bit too much, but surely the love god would take pity on him.

"That's it. Keep going straight."

Aki took a step.

"I said straight, not left!"

Aki's foot caught on something, and he fell. He braced for the fall, but his eyes opened. The black-and-white cat scurried away, and then he caught sight of the rock. His mouth dropped open. It was impossible. He was meant to be with Nao, and because of some stupid cat, he wouldn't.

Nao laughed. "The cat sat right in your path, and I tried to direct you away, but you ended up walking right into it."

Aki's chest ached. He wouldn't find love with Nao or anyone else. He would be alone forever because he failed.

Nao squatted and scratched behind the cat's ear. "Maybe you can buy a charm and ward off the bad luck."

The sticky air clung to Aki's skin, and with it all the bad lucky-in-love energy. Nao was right; a charm was the only way to combat it.

"Please, allow me purchase one quickly?" Aki pleaded. It was his duty to stay by Nao's side.

"Get one if you want."

Nao continued to lavish affection on the stray cat, as if rewarding it for getting in Aki's way. He had been visiting a lot more shrines with Nao, so perhaps another god would take pity on his misfortune.

Aki rounded the corner, but Detective Yamada had already found them. He couldn't abandon Nao while being questioned, and if Aki ran off, it would look suspicious. He scurried back to Nao.

Nao crossed his arms as Yamada approached. He wore simple pleated khaki pants and a white dress shirt that matched his graying hair.

"So the hand belonged to someone who wouldn't pay for protection?" The deep wrinkles on Yamada's forehead creased with his words.

"What good would they be to us without a hand to hand over the cash? We were here for the festival, just like everyone else. I don't see you accusing any of them."

"Come on, Mr. Murata. You know why."

"Then you'd know the Matsukawa doesn't play lap dog with the police anymore. You'd get a better response interrogating that cat than me."

The black of Aki's shoes against the ancient stone path resembled the darkness within a pool of blood. His muscles tensed.

"That cat likes you," Yamada said.

"I'm a cat person."

Yamada leaned over and looked at Aki. "The cat put the hand on your shoe, Mr. Hisona. Was it a peace offering, or was it bringing back something you left?"

"I've never met that cat before."

"Last time we had a chat, you cooperated easily. Don't be so hasty. Tell me everything you know about what happened. Then we can take care of this whole thing today."

Aki swallowed. Somehow, the look in Yamada's eyes told Aki he wasn't talking about the hand, but what happened with Shoda.

The alleyway might've had cameras.

Of course it had cameras. They were everywhere in the city. Aki looked away.

Yamada already knew what had happened. He'd probably waited for some other crime to occur before he raided headquarters to plant the evidence. If the police caught a yakuza for a crime against an innocent civilian, it would look better than catching yakuza fighting amongst themselves.

"Who does the hand belongs to?" Yamada asked.

Nao laughed. "This has to be your average psycho. We know how to clean up our messes."

Aki's muscles tightened underneath Yamada's gaze. He knew everything. All the police dotted around glared at him, because they knew, too. He'd killed Shoda. They only needed Shoda's body to charge him with murder, and since it was missing, it could turn up anywhere.

Yamada stepped forward. "You got something you want to say, son?"

Aki had once volunteered to take the blame for an incident to cover for a higher-up yakuza. All the officers knew he wasn't the real criminal, but they still threw him around and kicked him for "not cooperating." What horrors would they unleash on him for a crime he had committed?

Aki rubbed his thumb over his hand. It was only a matter of time before he'd be arrested. If things got too dire, he'd turn himself in to avoid getting the family in trouble for some trumped-up charge.

Nao half stepped in front of Aki. "Did we answer all your questions already?"

Yamada gave a knowing grin. "For now."

"Then you can get the fuck away from us."

CHAPTER 07

• • •

AKI OPENED HIS eyes in the moonlight-filled night.
Shit.

He had meant to take only a short nap before searching for Shoda, but he'd completely dozed off.

A layer of sweat slickened his skin and glued the futon blanket to his chest. Even though he couldn't remember his dreams, his head still spun, and a sour taste refused to leave his mouth.

Musk lingered on the blankets alongside the scent of jasmine from the laundry detergent. He peeled them off and slipped on his glasses, not wanting to bother putting in his contacts. Fuse's futon was laid out, but he wasn't there. Aki yawned. It was best to start searching for Shoda and then ask the house recruits about him if Aki couldn't find any sign of the body.

Nobu meowed outside.

Stupid Kohta couldn't remember to feed her. Aki pulled on a robe and opened the door. The hairless cat rubbed against his leg before trotting across the hall to Nao's office.

Light crept out from under the door, and then came a faint scream. The past always haunted Nao in his dreams.

Aki glanced down at the cat. "Let's wake him up."

He opened the door, spilling light into the hallway before closing it behind them. When the workday was finished, Nao would always take a bath then ditch his suit for a yukata robe. He looked more alluring in them anyway.

A small stream of moans left Nao's parted lips as he slept on the sofa. A business book lay across his chest. Then he thrashed. It opened his indigo yukata and exposed the sides of his chest.

Aki licked his lips. One day he'd have the courage to kiss Nao awake from his nightmares.

"Murata," Aki said.

Nao's eyes shot open as he jerked awake.

"I'm sorry for entering without permission, but you were…"

It was better for Nao not to know he screamed out in terror most nights. He rubbed his eyes while Aki sat on the coffee table.

"You always looked cuter in glasses. Is that why you don't wear them around the others?" Nao bit his lip and shook his head. "Excuse me, it's been a long day."

Aki's heart thumped against his ribs. If he followed Nao's gaze correctly, he was staring at Aki's chest. Though he'd slipped the robe on, he'd left it open, hoping Nao would look. But Aki could never tell what Nao thought behind his stare. Did he find the mismatched skin alluring, or did he stare in disgust?

"Where do you think the hand came from?" Nao asked.

"It's hard to say."

Nobu purred in the silent room as Aki scratched up her spine. She stretched and jumped on Nao's chest and rubbed against the book until Nao pushed it under the sofa to prevent it from falling. He yawned and petted the cat's cheek. He glanced at Aki then frowned.

"What happened?" Nao asked.

Of course, Aki had washed off the makeup he wore to hide his bruised face when he took his bath.

"The match at the gym," Aki said.

"But I told Hiro not to hit your face."

"It was before. When I went the first time."

Aki pressed his fingers along his face, pushing the dull ache to a sharp pain. Nao's eyebrows drew together, and he stopped stroking the cat.

He stared into Aki's eyes, but not the way he would during the day. There was nothing poking or prodding in Nao's gaze, but gentle caresses that stopped time, like his arms finally wrapped around Aki in a lover's hug. Aki's tongue tingled. If he could he would fall to his knees and confess everything. But Shoda was the miracle recruit. The one who, even as he scrubbed the floors, Nao could see the potential for greatness in.

Aki was no one to Nao. Just someone he shoved into a room and made moan so he could sneak out. All Aki could do was make tea and kill his friend. No wonder Nao stopped the brief touches they shared. Aki never deserved them in the first place.

The back of Aki's throat ached, and water welled up in his eyes. He rubbed the tears away but left his glasses on. They were the only shield between him and Nao. If Aki took them off, he would cry and confess it all, but even with all his loyalty, he couldn't bear the punishment. He wasn't strong enough to face the agony of being separated from Nao.

Aki had no one. His relationships formed when he drank sake with Nao and became a full-fledged Matsukawa. Without them, he would die alone and would be found only after the neighbors complained about the smell. He might as well jump off the Kiyomizu Temple than confess and be forced to leave the family.

Aki grabbed the edge of the coffee table, grounding himself to the world.

He was real.

The table was real.

He hadn't been forced out of the family yet, and as soon as he burned Shoda's corpse, he wouldn't have to worry anymore.

Aki's knuckles ached, but he couldn't let go or he'd float away. His chin quivered. He wouldn't leave this world.

Nao cleared his throat. "What made you want to try fighting in the first place?"

"I—I've been training a month. It was time."

"A bag is a lot different than a person."

"I realize that now." Aki bit his lip to keep it from trembling.

"Do we have time in tomorrow's schedule for a trip to the country for a few hours?"

"Besides your daily activities, nothing is planned before seeing the harvest moon viewing event at the Daikakuji Temple."

"Good. We'll go out after lunch." Nao scooped Nobu in his arms and stood. "It's time for bed."

Aki bowed. "Of course."

"Try to get back to sleep, Aki, even if the house does creak."

As long as Nao kept on intimately using his first name, Aki would hold on to the hope that Nao would see him as someone more than a loyal servant.

"Good night."

Aki followed Nao outside the office. He placed Nobu on the floor and closed the bedroom door behind him. She pawed underneath it for a second but then stopped and stared out the window as if she saw a ghost.

The time between midnight and one, the veil separating the worlds thinned. If Shoda's spirit wanted revenge, it would be the best hour to strike.

Aki sighed. He shouldn't allow his superstitions to get the best of him. All he needed to do was find Shoda's body and give it a proper send-off into the other world. He owed Shoda that as a friend. Aki would've wanted the same for himself if he had ended up on the wrong end of a knife.

If nothing happened to the body at the gym, then it must be somewhere around headquarters. Aki took a flashlight from the kitchen and slipped outside.

A concrete fence surrounded the Matsukawa complex. Its high walls cut off the glare of the dotted streetlights, leaving only the moon and Aki's dinky flashlight to cut through the darkness.

The soft shuffle of Aki's shoes against the gravel path echoed in his ears. The air tingled with humidity, and the damp smell of the carport left a metallic taste in the back of Aki's throat. He examined the car, but nothing was amiss.

He narrowed his eyes at a groove formed in the path. There were no tire marks or footprints. So someone must've dragged

Shoda's body behind him. Or it could've been left by a recruit lugging the recyclables out.

Aki rubbed his temple. He wasn't an investigator. It would be impossible to figure out where Shoda was hiding with only some marks in dirt.

But he couldn't give up.

Aki followed the tracks since there was nothing else to go on.

Each time he took a step, the pebbles beneath him crunched. After a few steps, the sound grew louder. The hairs on the back of his neck stood on end, and the metallic feeling in his mouth returned like a blade had kissed his tongue.

He stopped and looked over his shoulder, but no one was there. He shook his head and continued following the tracks. They headed to the shed toward the back of the compound. Yet with each step, there came a delay in the grind of pebbles.

Something was wrong. He could feel it. Something or someone was following him, but when he looked, nothing was there. Aki's heart thumped harder in his chest. He tried to steady his breath, but it hitched inside of him.

It had to be Shoda coming back to seek his revenge.

Aki broke into a run, but the footsteps followed.

He glanced over his shoulder, and a white orb hunted him.

CHAPTER 08
• • •

AKI DARTED AROUND the cars, but the white orb of Shoda's spirit chased him. Aki's shallow gasps left the edges of his vision blurred. Without finding rest, Shoda's spirit would roam the Earth seeking vengeance.

Heat swelled in a single point along Aoi's spine, no doubt from where Shoda's gaze bore into him. The footsteps grew louder with each step closer to the shed.

Shoda's breathing cut through the air. His energy must've grown strong enough to pierce through to the living world. He was going to finish what he started.

His footsteps gained on Aki. Then he was shoved to the ground.

"Please, Shoda, listen," Aki called out.

"You know where Shoda is?"

Aki opened his eyes, and it wasn't Shoda at all, but Fuse. Even in the dull light coming from their flashlights, Aki would recognize that bald head anywhere.

"What are you doing out at night?" Aki asked.

"I'm on night duty. What are you doing here?"

"The cat woke me up."

"Why are you outside, then?"

Aki bit his tongue. "I thought I saw Shoda."

Fuse frowned. "So you haven't seen him all day either?"

"Not since we went drinking."

Aki's fingers dug into the gravel.

The stench of damp wood lingered in the air with a putrid undertone. Something was in the shed.

"Shoda still hasn't texted back since this morning. It's not like him," Fuse said. "Did it seem like he'd do something like this?"

"We split when he met some lady."

"You think he's been fucking some girl for twenty-four hours? She must be really good, eh?"

"Yeah…" Aki stood and brushed the dirt off his robe. "Maybe he got sick of waiting around for his promotion."

"You think?"

"It's the easiest explanation."

"Maybe he ran into one of the Koreans coming back. Kurosawa looked like he was out for blood when he came by," Fuse said.

"I don't think—"

"Or maybe the bitch was crazy, drugged him, took his money, and dumped him in the forest. Or worse, she was as nuts as Murata and fucking chopped off his hand and dumped it off at the shrine for a cat toy."

"I guess it could be true." If it kept Fuse away, Aki would go along with his crazy idea.

Fuse's brow furrowed, and he twirled the flashlight in his hand. "Shoda talked about wanting to send money home to his family."

"Then he might've cut out and got a job at a construction site."

"Maybe—"

"Being an unpaid apprentice is hard. If Shoda needed the money now, then he wouldn't stick with the family, even if everyone thought he was perfect. I barely had enough money to afford paper until Nao made me his secretary."

Every time Shoda's name rolled from Aki's tongue, the moldy smell grew stronger. He was sure Shoda's body was in the shed. Aki put his hand under his nose to filter the smell and block the urge to gag.

Fuse dug his shoe into the ground. "Me and Shoda would joke about you—how you'd get up in the middle of the night because Murata needed a bedtime blow job. I know Shoda was jealous, but neither of us envied what you have to do to keep your position."

Aki's hands curled into a fist around a pebble. It dug into his palm in a welcoming pain. "It's fine."

Fuse whistled. "You think Murata's ever going to get a wife? Then he'd at least get his own place, and you wouldn't have to watch your ass when he's around."

"He doesn't seem to care about that stuff."

Fuse shrugged. "He's gotta have a kid to carry on his family name."

"I think Murata will do whatever he wants," Aki said, his voice flat.

"He's probably too much of a homo to even consider it."

The only person in the family who knew Aki liked men was Nao. Aki had hoped with a gay godfather homophobic slurs wouldn't happen, but it made them something whispered behind Nao's back, instead. Aki let the others think whatever they wanted about him. It was easier that way.

Aki ground his teeth together. "You should get back to work. I have to wax the car."

"Wax?"

"Murata thinks he saw a scratch and wanted to get it done. I ended up falling asleep. So now I have to find a car-detailing place or do it myself."

Fuse laughed. "You're going to do it in your robe?"

"I wanted to check if we had some here before getting dressed." Aki pointed to the shed. "If not, I'm heading out."

"I don't think we have any."

"Then I'll be gone for a few hours."

"Good luck, man."

Aki waited until Fuse walked out of sight before taking the last few steps to the shed. The wax lie was a perfect excuse to explain his absence.

The smell of death lingered in the air. It had to be Shoda's body in the shed. Aki opened the creaking door, and the full blast of the stench hit him. He winced from the smell.

Once it dissipated, he shined his flashlight inside.

No Shoda.

Not even some other body was there, only a bloody tarp.

Fuck.

CHAPTER 09

· · ·

KUROSAWA'S MUSCLED bulk made the chair he sat in appear small. His cropped hair drew out the crow's feet around his eyes, and as he spoke to the house leader, the skin on his forehead creased.

Aki listened behind the doorway and gnawed on his lower lip as fragments of the conversation emerged.

"Hand…"

"…Shoda…"

"Not like him…"

"…missing…"

"…body…"

Aki had spent all morning asking the newer recruits if they had seen anything or done any special work around Nao's car. They would've been doing Aki a favor if they had already disposed of the corpse, but none of them said they had. Then he'd asked if they'd seen Shoda to cover up any inkling his questioning might've brought up.

The conversation continued.

"…body…"

"He saw him."

Aki's eyes widened. Had one of the recruits ratted him out? Aki cleared his throat and stepped into the room, ending the conversation.

"Father Murata is ready to see you now," he said.

"Let's not keep him waiting." Kurosawa walked over, and his sheer size dwarfed Aki.

He couldn't read the expression on Kurosawa's face, but it didn't matter. Whatever the reason he called for an emergency meeting couldn't be good. Hopefully what he needed to say wouldn't permanently cancel the pleasant country tour Nao had planned.

Kurosawa's heavy steps on the stairs were like a bear chasing Aki. He rubbed his palm. He'd find Shoda, somewhere.

They entered Nao's office.

The morning tea, a deep astringent oolong for the surprise meeting, still sat on Nao's desk. He had to have been deep in thought to not finish. He and Kurosawa exchanged formal greetings before he sat on one of the sofas.

"I hope this isn't anything too serious," Nao said. "That hand didn't have anything to do with us, did it?"

"There's no new information about the hand," Kurosawa said.

Aki scooted to the farthest seat. Nao had a habit of mentioning calling people during a meeting, but being the technophobe he was, he'd forget to tell Aki to make the calls. Since then, Aki sat in all the meetings taking notes of the tasks he needed to do. He opened the end-table drawer beside him and grabbed a stack of papers.

Nao cocked an eyebrow. "Are there any signs of the Korean mob?"

"You still have them too scared to come anywhere near Kyoto."

"There's no telling how long that will last."

Aki listened as he folded what had to be his five hundredth crane since Shoda died. It had been more than he ever made in such a short time, but the mild distraction kept his thoughts from racing.

"Then why are you here?" Nao asked.

"I got more information on the blood splatter—"

"What blood splatter?"

"I called about it yesterday."

Nao glared at Aki, and he bit his lip. "Forgive me. With everything going on, it slipped my mind."

Kurosawa crossed his arms. "That's convenient, because some of the information is about you."

Nao took a sip of tea, and the cup hid all the expression on his face. Aki's fingers glided over the crease in the paper. His stomach could fold a thousand cranes in one go with the amount it twisted.

Would it be better to confess or see what Kurosawa knew? No one had seen the fight, but someone knew Shoda's body had been in the trunk of Nao's car, and Aki was the only one allowed to drive it.

Kurosawa crossed his arms. "Seems like you were hitting up the bars the other night."

Aki licked his lips and nodded.

"You were with Shoda."

"Fuse came, too. Eventually some women we met tagged along with us," Aki said, trying to hold his voice steady.

"What were you doing?"

"Celebrating my promotion. It was the first time all three of us had the night off."

"You were the last to see Shoda."

So Kurosawa must've spoken to Fuse. Aki ran his fingers through his hair. Kurosawa must've wanted to trap Aki and squeeze a confession out of him.

Nao cleared his throat, getting Kurosawa's attention. "What does this have to do with the bloodstain?"

The crease in Kurosawa's forehead returned. "Why don't you ask him?"

"What are you insinuating about my secretary?"

Aki's ears grew hot. Someone might've seen. Kurosawa could have the security footage of the fight in his jacket pocket. Nao would lose face the moment he pulled it out. No matter how much Aki's throat ached or his insides crumpled, nothing came out.

"You think the bloodstain belongs to Shoda?" Nao asked.

"He was an ideal candidate, and now he's gone. Usually the last person..." Kurosawa said.

"And the hand?"

"Shoda didn't have a record, and the police weren't able to identify the prints. But they're usually the last to piece everything together."

"So the hand is Shoda's?"

"Who else could it be?" Kurosawa shrugged.

Nao groaned and rubbed his forehead. "Did you use to be a cop, Kurosawa? Because you're worse than Detective Yamada when it comes to pointing fingers."

Aki held his breath. He didn't deserve Nao defending him. He finished the bright-red crane and grabbed the next from the stack.

White.

The color of death.

Kurosawa turned back to Aki. "Did you see anyone else around when you two parted ways?"

The hairs on the back of Aki's neck stood on end. Nao's keen gaze looked upon him, but behind the stone face of the yakuza boss was the intimacy they shared.

Aki bent the head of the crane.

No.

He was imagining all of it.

Nao didn't care about him.

"Perhaps there was security footage," Aki said.

Kurosawa shook his head. "Those old yakuza bars know better. So you didn't see anyone suspicious when you parted ways? Because you're the last hope."

"Not anyone I can recall."

Nao shrugged. "See, Shoda probably couldn't deal with being a yakuza and left. It's exactly why I pushed apprenticeship back to a year."

"You were telling me you were impressed by him last week," Kurosawa said.

"He's nothing but a deserter now. All these guys join and they think they'll be making the big bucks in under a year, when it takes at least five to get comfortable. Shoda had potential, but he didn't have patience."

Kurosawa pointed to Aki. "He apprenticed less than six months before you drank sake with him. Maybe if you did that with Shoda, we'd still have him."

"Aki's different. He gave me special help."

Kurosawa raised a brow, and Aki dropped his crane into the basket. His movements became more fluid with the next one.

"Yamada will be looking for someone to pin something on since that hand popped up," Kurosawa said.

"Not every body part can be us. Remember that lady in Tokyo? Cut up her ex-boyfriend and left his body parts all over the house."

"Excuse me for interrupting," Aki said. "But, Father Murata, if you still wanted to go to the country and see the Otsukimi moon-viewing festival, then we need to leave soon."

Nao stood. "We need to get going. See you later tonight."

Unlike the dragon festival, Aki was forced to share Nao with all the higher-ups in the family joining him for the Otsukimi festival.

"Double-check the wards are keeping their eyes out," Nao said then turned to Aki. "Give me a few minutes. I'll meet you downstairs."

Aki nodded, his chest filled with warmth. Their quiet excursion out of the city together was more important than whatever Kurosawa made up.

Nao drifted into his bedroom while Aki escorted Kurosawa downstairs. Pampas grass and a serving of fifteen white tsukimi dango rice dumplings were stacked on a plate by the entry vestibule. The house recruits had prepared the house for the autumn full moon, but Nao wouldn't have it any other way.

Kurosawa took longer than necessary to put on his shoes. "You forgot to tell Father Murata about the bloodstain. There seems to be something you're not telling us. It is a bit suspicious."

Aki bowed, and more lies spilled from his mouth. "I'm sorry for my forgetfulness, but there's nothing to say."

"I know recruits lining up for your cushy job of answering phones." Kurosawa puffed out his chest. "I can put someone through tea school, and he could easily replace you if you step out of line."

"There's more to being Father Murata's secretary than making tea and answering phones."

Aki had to balance Nao's schedule, too.

Kurosawa's eyes narrowed. "What did Shoda say to you?"

"Congratulations."

"What did he say before he disappeared?"

The tone in Kurosawa's voice made it clear there was more he hadn't told Nao.

Aki gulped then opened his mouth to speak.

"Why are you still here?" Nao asked before Aki could get out a word. "And no one else can make tea like Aki, besides myself, of course."

Aki's cheeks grew hot as Kurosawa pulled out a piece of paper from his pocket.

"Then you might want to look at this, then, before you hold your secretary to such high esteem."

CHAPTER 10

• • •

KUROSAWA PUSHED the paper into Nao's free hand. His eyes darted over the text, and then his brows knitted together.

A chill shot down Aki's spin. Whatever was on the note couldn't be good, but if it was reliable information, Kurosawa would've brought it up before.

Nao rubbed his thumb along the handle of his briefcase then glanced toward Kurosawa. "Find out more, and we'll talk about it tonight."

"I'll do my best, but—"

"I didn't ask for your best," Nao snapped.

Aki had never seen the monster lurking inside Nao emerge outside a boxing ring. But a fire had been lit in his eyes, and a sinister expression washed over his face, leaving no doubt the monster who haunted Nao's dreams had escaped.

Aki gulped.

Kurosawa took a step back, his face turning pallid. Even the cockiest man would cower when facing that Nao.

"Of course, Father Murata." Kurosawa bowed. "Forgive the slip of my tongue."

"It's not your tongue I have the problem with."

"I'll get on this right away."

Nao shoved the note in Kurosawa's face. "Don't come tonight unless you have something to report."

Kurosawa bowed and left.

Nao's expression softened, but the glint behind his eyes wasn't from the Nao Aki knew. Aki always thought Nao restrained the killer inside of him, but perhaps it was the other way around.

"Don't let Kurosawa get to you," Nao said. "He's still a homophobic bastard even if he pretends he isn't."

"I, ah—"

"Let's get going."

Nao opened the front door and didn't stop his quick pace until he arrived at the car. Only after putting the briefcase in the trunk did he slow enough for Aki to fulfill his duty and open the door. They got in, and Nao gave a vague set of directions only someone who never drove before would give.

Aki ran his sweaty palms along the steering wheel. Whatever was on the note disturbed Nao so much he did nothing but stare out the window. Maybe someone did see the fight and wrote a note about the incident.

No.

It was silly.

No one had been there. If anything, it was the guy from the gym reporting the blood in Nao's car.

If anything, the keys to the car were kept alongside the others at headquarters. Aki could deny all knowledge and suggest someone had gotten the keys and shoved Shoda's body in the trunk.

Then it would be another lie he'd tell Nao. They weren't supposed to roll off his tongue so easily, especially when thinking of excuses to tell Nao. Aki picked at the stitching on the steering wheel. Nao demanded loyalty above everything else, and if Aki couldn't keep to the standard, then Nao would find someone to replace him.

"Turn off here," Nao said.

A cedar forest grew around them, and soon the paved road scattered to gravel as Aki drove up the mountain.

"Park here. We'll need to walk the rest of the way."

Aki followed the instructions and came around to open Nao's door. The glare in his eyes had disappeared, and somehow in the countryside of Kyoto, Nao's whole appearance brightened.

Nao opened the trunk, and the image of Shoda's body flashed in Aki's mind. There had been so much blood on the sidewalk. Anyone with half a brain could have noticed it on the bumper. Nao grabbed the briefcase and closed the trunk, banishing Shoda from Aki's imagination.

Aki swallowed, but the lump in his throat stayed.

"You got some paper?" Nao asked.

A stack of origami paper was tucked away in the glove compartment in case Aki ran out at a location. He placed a few sheets in his pocket.

"Come on," Nao said, heading down a trail.

The pollen grew thick as they hiked up the mountain. Aki sniffed and rubbed his eyes while the birds chirped in the late-afternoon sun. Allergy-inducing trees aside, stepping away from the city reminded Aki of the times he'd picked up an origami book and created a dragon or Venus flytrap. Though it took more effort, the novelty of a new project was welcomed.

Minutes passed, and as they climbed, Aki's eyes itched and his nose tingled. A part of him wanted to go back to enjoying Nao's company in the city, where he could breathe. Just like how no other paper creature unfurled Aki's innermost wishes like the cranes could.

"This is a good spot," Nao said.

He opened the briefcase. From the inscription on the lock, Aki recognized it was the one Sakai, the head of the legal side of the Matsukawa, had given him. But then a shiver ran down Aki's spine. Instead of business papers, Nao's briefcase held a gun. Aki had never seen one before since the simple act of possession would land the owner six years in jail. Even the yakuza didn't play around with carrying one unless necessary.

"Let me have one of those papers," Nao said while screwing on a silencer.

Aki pulled out a red paper with golden swirls. He ran his fingers through his hair as Nao pinned the paper to a tree.

Nao wouldn't do anything like the blood-filled, life-ending thoughts flashing in Aki's mind. He'd only wanted some shooting practice. Nothing more, right?

The tingling in Aki's nose migrated to his extremities. He rubbed his shoe against the forest floor of dead leaves in a vain attempt to make the numbness stop.

Nao slowly loaded the bullets into the gun's magazine. He could've been sipping tea and possess the same expression.

"A lot of people in the family wonder why I haven't chosen a bodyguard yet," Nao said. "Do you know why?"

"It wouldn't be my place to say."

"It's just us, so speak your mind."

"You haven't found someone else you like enough to be around you all day?"

Nao laughed. "You know me too well. But that's half the story."

"What's the other half?"

"I don't need one while I remain in Kyoto. Take a guess why?" Nao asked.

Aki's knees wobbled as the numbness took them over. The birds' song subsided as if they wanted to hear his response, too. He stared at Nao's gun.

"No one would dare go against you," Aki said.

"Exactly." Nao popped the magazine into the gun and loaded a bullet into the chamber.

The air thinned, or maybe the pollen finally won against Aki. He swallowed. Why did Nao drag him out into the middle of the woods with a loaded gun and ask questions of betrayal?

Nao continued, "I built up a reputation. Everyone sees me in the boxing ring five days a week. No one comes close to beating me. It plants a seed of hesitation for anyone even thinking of double-crossing me."

Nao held the gun up, securing it with both hands, then pulled the trigger.

Aki jumped.

Even with the silencer, the sound popped in Aki's ears long after. The paper target had a hole exactly in the center.

A grin spread across Nao's face. "I was thinking I would need more practice after the infection screwed up my arm, but I guess not."

"G-good shot."

"You know I'm just as safe walking the streets in the middle of the Korean territories. Can you guess why?"

"Because of what you did to them?"

"The rumors probably have me killing a hundred of them by now, but no." Nao sighed. "I owe the Korean leader a favor. He wouldn't let anything bad happen to me until I pay it back."

"Because he brought you back to headquarters when you were injured?"

"I wanted to die, and he forced me to live."

A vise around Aki's heart tightened until each thump pulsed throughout his body, turning his numbness into sheer agony. Nao had too much to live for to wish for death. He had Aki.

Nao shook his head, his hair covering his face. "My point is you need to show people you can rip them to shreds so they won't cross you."

"But I'm just a secretary."

"You're my secretary." Nao handed Aki the gun, but he only stared at it. "Take it."

"I—"

"Technically you're my first line of defense if someone does try to start something. You train at the gym; you also need to train at this."

It was impossible. He couldn't shoot. He could barely defend himself. Nao was mistaken.

Aki bit his lip. "I was never taught... The war happened and—"

"That's why we're here."

Nao guided Aki's hand to the gun, and the warmth in Nao's touch eased his frantic thoughts. Aki grasped the gun. The weight pulled at his wrist more than he thought it would.

"Good. See, it's not too bad, is it?"

Aki's ears grew hot. Even the smallest of Nao's praises folded away Aki's anxiety. It was more pathetic than anything, but Aki didn't care. Nao thought he did a good job.

Nao's breath tickled Aki's ear as he stood behind him. "Can you spread your legs a bit for me, Aki?"

Of course he'd spread them any time Nao wanted. Aki followed the instructions even if the fantasy of Nao and himself naked in the woods grew steamier by the second.

"A little wider."

A small moan left the back of Aki's throat, and Nao chuckled.

"Aim," Nao ordered.

Aki held up the gun.

"We're not in some flashy yakuza movie. Use both hands to stabilize the gun. One bullet, one kill. Then you don't have to spend so much time digging around for the bullet."

Then Nao's hands were over Aki's, putting the gun into a proper hold. Aki's cock stirred. The chirping of the birds and the buzz of bugs disappeared. The gun that he didn't want to touch moments before, Aki grew to love, because it led Nao to finally put his hands on him again. With the sizzling caress of Nao's fingers around his, Aki could fold a million cranes to honor each digit.

There was no missing body, no note spelling out Aki's fate, no police detective ready to pounce on him. There was only Nao.

"Remember what you told me that night," Nao whispered. "How some days you have to touch something to remember that you're real? Well, Aki, this gun is real, and the life you might have to take when you pull is real. Fire!"

Aki squeezed the trigger.

The shock of the blast filled his arms, and even with the silencer he lost his hearing. In the quiet seconds, the hot gun grew cold. Slowly the chirping birds returned, but Nao's touch was absent along with the top-right corner of the paper target.

"Do it again," Nao said, though his voice seemed farther away.

Aki shot again, but winced before pulling the trigger. The paper wasn't even hit.

"You're expecting it this time. So you move. Take in a breath and let it out as you pull the trigger. Don't think, just do."

Aki tried to repeat the steps, but without Nao's deep voice in his ear and laced fingers to guide Aki's movements, he failed. Even after another three attempts, he missed them all.

Aki bowed. "Please forgive me. I'll try harder."

Nao shook his head. "Sometimes I look at you and think you're too sweet to be in the Matsukawa."

"I used to be in a motorcycle gang."

"Really?" Nao crossed his arms.

"I mean, we called ourselves a gang, but we just illegally modified the bikes so they'd be louder and didn't go the speed limit."

Nao laughed. "No wonder you passed your driving test the first go. You already had your motorcycle license."

"Driving comes easy to me. Almost as much as making cranes."

"How did you get in with that crowd?"

Aki crunched a few leaves under his shoe but didn't speak, and Nao didn't either. Nao leaned forward, his eyes alert, waiting for Aki to open up. It was nice that Nao cared to know, but it wasn't like Fuse and Aki stayed up at night talking about their past while reading magazines. Aki didn't really speak about it much.

"I was raised by my grandparents most of my life." Aki took in a deep breath and looked away from Nao. "My grandfather was brought over from Korea during the war and fell in love with a Japanese woman. He died when I was thirteen, and she followed soon after."

"So your parents were no good?"

Aki bit his lip. "There was a reason I didn't live with my mother until I had to. I changed schools, then made some friends who cared more about motorcycles than how odd my skin looked. The speed helped me forget. Like if I drove fast enough I could outrun what happened."

Nao nodded along.

"Most of my friends ended up joining the yakuza, but I tried to stay straight. But then I got fired from that furniture-assembly job for making the office chairs backwards, so I ended up joining as well."

"It worked out for the best."

"Shoda was the only one who hadn't quit."

"He has now."

Aki looked up into the canopy. "Yeah… One who quit ended up joining the Osaka police department. It's a little hard to believe."

"You don't talk to that one anymore, do you? He'd probably find some way to plant something on you."

"Of course not."

"Good. I'll teach you how to use a knife next time." Nao gestured to the place on Aki's face where he covered his bruise with makeup. "You're not so good with your fists, but at least you're good with your hands."

"I don't understand."

"Those cranes you always make. You could do a dozen a minute. Maybe a knife is the way you should go. Have you been in a knife fight before?"

Aki swallowed and shook his head. What he'd done with Shoda wasn't a fight.

Nao smiled. "You'd probably be good at it. Have you decided who those cranes are for yet?"

"I haven't."

Nao brushed past him. "When you have a thousand of them, you'll figure it out."

CHAPTER 11

• • •

NIGHT DESCENDED as Aki drove back to the city.

People flooded the streets around the temple for the moon-viewing festival and accompanying boat ride. Aki had to park far away, but he didn't mind. It meant he could share a few more precious moments alone with Nao.

The autumn moon hung closer than before and shined down brighter than any streetlight. They strolled in silence, passing families in street clothes and others in traditional yukata.

"On nights like tonight, I miss wearing yukata," Nao said.

"There might be a shop—"

Nao shook his head. "No. Suits are my uniform now. Only when the day's work is done can I slip one on."

"I understand."

"When we get there, don't let Kurosawa talk shit about you."

"But—"

"Don't worry so much about rank when people start pointing fingers. Silence is its own confession."

Aki bit his tongue. Breaking the formality of rank would disturb the harmony of the family, but if Nao wished it…

Aki rubbed his thumb over his knuckles. His silence around Kurosawa had been a confession, but everything he hinted at was true. Once he put together the pieces, there'd be no way Aki could continue along Nao's side.

"Hey." Nao stopped, his eyebrows drawn together. "Your job is very important, and I meant what I said to him. It would be impossible for someone to replace you."

Aki's cheeks flushed. Nao hadn't said that to Kurosawa at all.

Nao held out his hand for a second, then awkwardly shoved it in his pocket. "Let's get going."

Aki could only nod and hope that Nao hadn't picked up on his anxiety. The second Nao learned what he'd done, Nao would take back his words.

Kurosawa and Sakai were waiting by the red torii gate, dressed in the same pristine suits Nao wore. The only difference between them was the absence of the family crest on Sakai's lapel. Sakai led the legal business side of the family, so he had a front to keep, even if his prosthetic pinkie gave away his yakuza roots.

"So you found something?" Nao asked.

Kurosawa cleared his throat and eyed Aki. "I think so."

"I told you not to come unless you were certain."

"I know, but—"

Nao rubbed his temple. "We'll talk about your insolence after the boat rides."

Darkness surrounded the shrine. The soft glow of paper lanterns and the full moon were the only guiding light. A musician played a disjointed melody on a string koto, luring the festivalgoers to the main stage. Once the other musicians joined in, the song became haunting, like a ghost unable to find peace.

Aki dared to step a little closer to Nao. If Kurosawa had a bombshell to drop, then Aki wanted to be beside Nao in his final hours. Aki would gladly accept whatever punishment was deemed necessary, but he would cherish each minute he still possessed with Nao.

"So beautiful," Nao said.

And it was.

The music swelled, and the shrine maidens dressed in their red and white period costumes were like stepping back in time.

He finally understood why Nao was in awe over the events. Aki could imagine him and Nao together, enjoying the same song being played centuries back. People stood where they stood year after year, and only in Kyoto could the same events on the same day happen for over a thousand years as if nothing had changed.

Shoda's problem had been his inability to see how Kyoto was worth protecting. He hadn't received a promotion because it wouldn't benefit the city. Nao only wanted to drink sake with yakuza who lived and died for the city and not for their own selfish pride.

The traditional music stopped, and the shrine maidens threw paper charms to the audience while a modern singer introduced herself. Her song spoke of love and heartache, but her words drifted like the ripples of the dragon boats gliding across the pond.

Nao wandered behind the stage where the golden boats waited for passengers. Kurosawa shook a driver's hand, planting a large sum of money to keep the boat private. The driver nodded, and the four men climbed in.

They rolled toward the center of the lake, joining a few other boats stationed there. A faint fishy smell lingered in the air due to the algae building up along the bank, but with the cicadas' singing accompanying the singer's more upbeat tune, it was quickly forgotten.

Since stepping onto the boat, Nao had only stared at the moon, while all Aki could do was gaze upon him. His delicate mouth and the way the moon made his skin glow stroked every inch of desire within Aki.

Things would be simpler if he could freeze time. He'd never let another second pass and would happily watch it until all his hair turned gray. Too bad it was impossible.

The boat operator lifted his pole, and it met the water with a thwack.

"Is something in the water?" Kurosawa asked.

"Happens when I hit dead fish," the operator said.

People in the boat a few yards beside them pointed their way. "Are you sure it's a fish?"

The pole stuck again, and the people in the other boat began to scream. A body floated beside the boat.

Nao groaned. "The second event ruined. How old is it?"

"Can't tell with the dark," Kurosawa said.

Aki covered his mouth. It was stupid to worry. No recruit would be stupid enough to dump Shoda in a lake. Aki bit the inside of his cheek and dared to lean over the edge.

He gasped.

It was Shoda.

And his hand was missing.

CHAPTER 12

AKI'S SKIN PRICKLED like a thousand papercuts. Since last night, whenever Aki entered a room people would stop their conversations. Kohta must've been spreading a rumor that Aki had dumped Shoda. Their eyes spoke of Aki's guilt even if their lips hadn't.

He bent the head to another crane, then dumped it with the others in an overflowing bin. A new sheet and more repetitious folds—he didn't even need to look for perfection. Whatever the number, the multicolored cranes he made doubled once Shoda's body surfaced the previous night, each one more worthless than the next—but he was more useless than all of them combined.

A yakuza who couldn't even dispose of a body correctly couldn't be considered worthy of the title.

Aki's nightmares had been filled with Shoda's bloated corpse drowning him or chasing him down the alley of his death. Worse were the sweet memories of their high school friendship turned putrid. There had been no escaping the despair; even when he'd prepared Nao's morning tea, Aki mentally folded bloody cranes of betrayal to distract his thoughts.

Nao hadn't spoken to him since last night, but it didn't matter. Aki should've been too ashamed to sit outside Nao's office and fold cranes like an honorable family member. Yet there he was.

Top fold.

Frog mouth to diamond fold.

Press and repeat.

He was a traitor for killing one of their own, even if it was an accident. He deserved the harshest punishment Nao could imagine. Yet though Nao was the man he should've been the farthest from, Aki couldn't bear to leave his side.

Still, someone had wanted Shoda discovered. Someone had taken the time to desecrate his body and dump the parts where he and Nao had visited. Aki ran his fingers through his hair. Kurosawa had said people would line up for Aki's job, and it was clear someone wanted him out of the picture. Before, Aki had doubted anyone would betray another member of the family, but if Shoda could attack out of sheer jealousy, anything was possible.

Aki flipped over the paper to create another wing.

Kohta had done nothing but complain since he'd joined. He'd talked on and on about how he helped Nao catch the traitor working with the Koreans, and how their close relationship meant he didn't have to spend his days scrubbing like the rest of the new recruits.

There were even a few instances in the past where Aki entered Nao's office to find Kohta causally on the sofa chatting it up with Nao like they were old buddies. Aki's fingernails dug into his palm. Kohta was the only other person Nao addressed by first name, and since he resembled Nao's dead lover, Nao wouldn't mind him around all day.

Aki slammed a new paper on his desk. It had to be Kohta. He never had the decency to stand and formally bow when greeting Aki. Kohta had a complete disregard of rank and everything the Matsukawa stood for. He didn't care about the city at all. He only wanted money so he could keep his body dripping in name-brand clothes. Of course he'd frame Aki to get his job.

Aki crumpled the crane and stood.

Kohta would pay.

It wasn't like Aki was chained to his desk during the day, and Nao had locked himself in the office since Aki had delivered the morning tea. The moon viewing at a different temple was the only scheduled event, and that was hours away.

Without any more body parts to hack off, Kohta had to be pretending to clean somewhere. He half-assed everything he did. He couldn't even chop up Shoda correctly, giving up after severing his hand.

The more Aki searched, the more it all became clear. The way Kohta had asked about his job after Shoda died had all been to size him up.

Aki's nostrils flared when he finally spotted Kohta squatting beside Nobu's litter box.

"Stupid cat. How can you piss so much in one day?" Kohta scooped another clump into a trash bag.

Aki crossed his arms. "Think of how many times you piss in one day."

"But cats aren't supposed to like water."

"You're supposed to bow when someone superior approaches."

"You want me to bow with a bag of crap?" Kohta asked.

"Well, that's what you are."

Kohta's lip curled. "I'm not crap."

Aki took a step forward, leaving no room for Kohta to escape. "You're the last one to join, so from where everyone stands, even Nobu's shit outranks you."

Kohta bowed. "There, you happy?"

The tone shot through Aki like a bullet. Kohta didn't deserve to be a member of the family. He didn't belong by Nao's side. It was Aki's job, and he wouldn't let some ex-prostitute with good looks take his place.

Adrenaline flushed through Aki's body, lubricating his muscles in warmth.

Aki kicked over the litter box. Some of pellets flew down the hallway, but most landed square on Kohta's Gucci shoes. His eyes grew cold as he glared at Aki.

"Pick it up," Aki said between clenched teeth.

"I'll get a broom."

"Do it with your hands."

The prick actually rolled his eyes.

"Now!" Aki yelled.

Kohta groaned but lifted his feet out of the litter mound before kneeling. He turned over the box and scooped the first handful of litter inside.

"You think you can get rid of me so easily? Murata doesn't care about you. The only reason he let you join was because you reminded him of his dead lover."

Kohta's hair fell over his shoulder. "I helped him out on his last case, too, just like you, Mr. Secretary."

"No one gave you permission to talk."

Kohta pressed his lips together and scooped up another handful. Aki ground his teeth together. Kohta was the most pathetic excuse for a new recruit the family had ever had.

"Why did you do it?" Aki asked.

Kohta didn't answer immediately, so Aki pounded his fist against the wall. "I asked you a question."

"Because you told me to scoop up the litter."

"No. What you did to Shoda!"

"I didn't do anything to him."

Aki tipped over the box again, spilling what Kohta had scooped inside. Kohta's lips flattened, and the pellets he held in his hand shifted through his fingers.

"Stop pretending!" Aki yelled.

"Why don't you tell me what you convinced yourself I did?"

"You dumped Shoda in the lake."

Kohta brows squashed together. "Why would I do that?"

"You think you're so smart, don't you? You want my job."

Kohta laughed. "Like I know how to make tea."

Aki shook his head. Kohta was trying to disrespect him.

"How could you do that to Shoda's body?" Aki said.

"I didn't kill Shoda."

"You're a lying sack of shit. You cut off Shoda's hand."

"Are you trying to pin this on me to make me leave?"

Aki crossed his arms. "You're the one trying to get me banished so you can take over my positon."

"Sure, I'd get all the ladies Nao—"

"You don't fucking deserve to call him by his first name."

Kohta held up his hands in surrender. "You can have him. I don't want to wait at the beck and call of some psychopath."

"Don't you fucking call him that! You stupid fuck. Wait until Murata hears what you did," Aki said.

"I didn't do anything—"

Aki opened his mouth to speak, but his phone rang. He pulled it out from his jacket pocket.

"Hello," Aki answered.

"Mr. Hisona?" The voice was familiar, but Aki couldn't place it. "Yes?"

"This is Detective Yamada. We need to chat. Why don't you come by the station?"

CHAPTER 13

·   ·   ·

AKI HAD MANAGED to talk Detective Yamada into meeting at a bar across town. Yamada hadn't pressed the issue, so perhaps he didn't have any hard evidence against Aki. He sighed. It was probably just as easy to arrest him at a bar. He could only hope his cooperation protected the family.

Condensation on Aki's beer pooled around the bottom of the bottle and saturated one of the paper cranes.

If only the past few days were paper, then Aki could fold them into something meaningful. He pushed the cranes away.

They were worthless.

He was worthless.

Nao would like Kohta better as a secretary anyway.

"You drinking that, or are you too busy playing with paper?" Yamada sat in the empty chair across from Aki. He took a swig of Aki's beer. "Not bad."

Yamada wasn't even wearing a tie. He must've been off duty. He couldn't arrest anyone while he was off duty, could he? Even then it wouldn't stop some other cop from busting into the bar to put Aki in handcuffs.

Yamada leaned back in his chair. "Last time we talked, it seemed like there was something you wanted to say, but Murata interrupted us."

Aki gulped.

He hadn't told Nao he was coming. It would be better if he disappeared than to bring shame to the family. He hadn't meant for things to get so out of hand, but since they were, someone had to pay. It might as well be him.

"Lucky that body fished up so now we know who the hand belongs to," Yamada said.

Aki pressed his lips together. Shoda didn't have any prints on file. He'd only ventured out to buy food, and he'd never done anything for the police to recognize his face. The police had no way of identifying him as anything more than the body that belonged to a hand.

"Things will be easier for you if you talk," Yamada said.

"I'm not sure what you mean."

"We can carry you out of here in handcuffs or go to your headquarters and take Murata instead."

Aki's muscles tensed. There had to have been a camera in the street that caught the fight, or else Yamada wouldn't have singled him out.

Yamada picked up one of the cranes. "You're pretty good at that. How long have you been at it?"

"Since I was little."

Aki's grandmother had shown him how to make his first crane when he was old enough to realize his hands were different than everyone else's.

"You make them a lot?" Yamada asked.

"I like to keep my hands occupied."

"So that body was one of the Matsukawa."

Aki bit the inside of his cheek and shrugged. "Who knows?"

"Did you mean to cut off his pinkie and miss? So you dumped him in the lake when he bled out?"

"We wouldn't do anything like that."

Yamada took a sip of beer and reached into his pocket. He pulled out a red paper crane in an evidence bag.

Aki stared at the crumpled red paper, then closed his eyes. They had him. There was no way he could escape. Footsteps echoed in his ears. Shoda's ghost must've been ready to come after him. Shoving a crane down Shoda's throat was the only way to connect Aki to the crime without an eyewitness.

"Maybe you can tell me about this?" Yamada asked.

"It's paper. Does that answer your question?" Nao said.

Aki's eyes shot open at the sounds of Nao's voice. Nao pulled up the chair beside him and sat, their knees touching. If it wasn't for that contact, Aki wouldn't believe Nao was even there.

"The crane was shoved so far down the guy's throat the water didn't even touch it."

"Maybe the guy liked to eat paper," Nao answered before Aki could even open his mouth.

"It looks a lot like the paper Mr. Hisona uses make those cranes."

"Like no one else could pick up origami paper from a store."

Yamada leaned forward and glared at Aki. "Someone saw you with him a few days ago. Did you shove the crane in his mouth before you dumped his body in the lake?"

"We went drinking, then split up when he met someone," Aki said.

Nao glared at Aki, then stood, scraping his chair against the floor. "You found nothing, or else you would've knocked down headquarters' door."

"Don't doubt we haven't." Yamada crossed his arms.

"You say that every time, and yet the Matsukawa still stands."

"It would be easier if you give up someone like last time."

"Is Aki being arrested?" Nao hissed.

"I would like to ask him a few more questions, alone."

"So he's detained?"

Yamada leaned back. "With you here, I think his answers might be a bit different."

Nao slammed his hand on the table then grabbed Aki's wrist with the other. A fire was in Nao's eyes, and it was as if Yamada had disappeared.

"Let's go," Nao said, keeping his hold on Aki. "If he really thought you were up to something, he'd make you answer them at the station."

Aki's arms blossomed with goose bumps with Nao's touch, even if it was just to drag him out of the bar.

"Don't think I'm done!" Yamada yelled after them.

Even outside Nao didn't let go. He led them down the block, cutting between buildings as his pace increased. Nao didn't loosen his grip until they were a good fifteen minutes away.

"What were you thinking!" Nao yelled, finally breaking their bond.

"He called and—"

"You don't talk to the police. Fuck! I can't even look at you I'm so pissed."

Aki's lip trembled. "Forgive me."

"You know how much you piss me off right now."

Aki dropped to his knees, his fingers grasping the concrete alley and his head touching the dirty ground. Aki couldn't even bear to look at Nao's shoes, and even if he did, the tears would've clouded his vision.

"I'm sorry," Aki pleaded.

The crunch of Nao's shoes against the dirt stopped. "Why the fuck did you even go when he called?"

"I—I didn't want the family to get in trouble. I didn't want him to come into headquarters."

"How many times does he have to say that before you realize it's an empty threat? He needs us more than we need him. We drove away the Korean mob from the city, not him."

Aki's hot breath bounced off the ground and hit back into his face. He pressed his lips together. Through his hair-covered eyes, Aki peeked up to Nao. All of his muscles were tense, and his pacing continued. Aki couldn't rise from his bow. Nao never told him he could, and Aki doubted his knees would be able to hold his trembling frame.

"First you scream at Kohta for no reason, then you run off to the police?" Nao said. "I don't want to see you for the rest of the day, understood?"

The silence that followed spoke of Nao wanting Aki's confirmation. He clutched his hands into fists and winced. His heart ached like Nao had personally ripped it out of his chest, shoved it into a shredder, then stomped on the pieces.

"W-whatever you d-desire." Pain swelled in the back of Aki's throat with his cracked words.

"There's no point going out. There might be another dead body you want to take the blame for. So I'll gaze at the moon in the tearoom."

Aki nodded, no longer trusting his voice to speak.

"When the moon can be seen, bring pu-erh tea along with two cups to the tearoom. Until then leave me alone."

CHAPTER 14

"I FAILED EVERYONE," Aki muttered.

He lay back on his futon and curled into a ball. The light of the day still dominated the twilight, but a descending darkness loomed overhead like a death threat.

What did it matter?

He hadn't seen Nao in hours.

A few times throughout the day, the thought of making some excuse to knock on Nao's office door crossed Aki's mind, but he knew better. He couldn't go against a direct order.

If he was lucky, Nao would only excommunicate him when he delivered the tea. For what he did, he deserved a full zetsuenjo. He deserved every yakuza in Japan to know about his failure and to be only met with hostility should he attempt to associate with any of them. Yet if he couldn't stay with Nao, then what did it matter if he couldn't join another group?

Aki swallowed. He could probably start the tea in another half hour. The moon would be out by then. He clutched the edge of the blanket and buried his face into the cotton fibers.

His stomach ached like a thousand cranes with razor wings all decided to take flight in it.

The door opened, but Aki didn't look. It wouldn't be Nao, so it wouldn't matter.

"Cat!" Fuse yelled, but within a few seconds, Nobu pawed at the blanket covering Aki's face.

Nao must've been ignoring her, too. Aki reached out and scratched behind her ear as Fuse stepped inside.

At first Aki hadn't been sure about a hairless cat, but the peach-like fuzz on Nobu was as soothing to pet as any cat. So she looked a little different, just like him. Maybe that was what Nao liked about them; they were both oddities.

"You must have over a thousand by now," Fuse said.

"Probably."

Aki stroked Nobu's side as she plopped beside him. She was a sucker for attention. She'd be lonely with him gone since none of the other family members paid much attention to her.

Fuse pushed away a few cranes that had missed the basket and sat beside Aki. Nobu looked up at Fuse, meowed, and went pack to rubbing against Aki's hand until he resumed petting. Aki gave a faint smile and mentally gave his goodbye to the cat. He'd miss her.

"Heard they found Shoda," Fuse said.

"Yeah, you were right."

"About what?"

"The woman he ran off with must've been crazy."

Unlike before, the lie was harder to say. The weight pressed down on Aki, and he knew he couldn't go on with it for long.

"To fucking stab him and dump him like that," Fuse said.

Aki flicked one of the loose cranes. "It's pretty messed up."

"She must've been one crazy bitch." Fuse's brows drew together, creating short lines across his bald head.

They sat in silence for a minute, only interrupted by Nobu's purring. Fuse petted her, but she squirmed away from his reach. She watched Aki toy with one of the cranes before pouncing on it and batting it to the other side of the room. Her pattering paws thumped across the wooden floor in her chase.

"Why would she cut off his hand?" Aki asked.

"Maybe she thought with Shoda's record, we'd be blamed for it."

Aki no longer thought Kohta had anything to do with it since Nao defended him. So maybe whoever took Shoda wasn't trying to get at Aki in particular but wanted to distract the police from another crime they committed. Or maybe it was a new recruit who screwed up entirely and didn't want to tell anyone his mistake. If he did own up eventually, the recruit's mistake would get back to Nao, and he could be pretty scary when angered.

Aki ran his fingers through his hair. Either way he was fucked. He hadn't played detective well enough and spent the last few hours at headquarters in an attempt to calm down.

Aki sighed. "Shoda didn't have a record. So it was pointless."

"He didn't?"

"He was a model recruit in every way. He could do a lot of things and get away with it more than someone with a record."

"Well, fuck me." Fuse laughed. "I thought both of you had one since you two were in that motorcycle gang together."

"We weren't much of a gang."

The police had Aki's prints. Could Aki's prints survive being shoved down Shoda's throat? Aki flicked another crane. There was no point trying to guess.

Fuse picked up the crane Aki messed with. "You leave these all over headquarters."

"And you leave your yakuza magazines all over the place."

"Everyone reads those. No one can do anything with your cranes."

"Whatever." Aki rolled over.

Fuse's laugh cut through Aki. He wanted to be left alone with his melancholy. In the silence, the razor-winged cranes took flight, and Aki couldn't even muster up a smile as he watched Nobu play.

Aki wasn't sure how long he watched, but when the door to Nao's office slammed shut, Aki rubbed his eyes. He was ready for judgment.

"I need to go." Aki stood.

"I know he's got a leash on you in more than one place."

Aki's eyes narrowed. "Father Murata is the boss. He's got a leash on everyone."

"Does he at least use protection with you? Who knows what kind of diseases those fags pick up?"

"Fuck you. Everyone's tired of your shit."

Fuse puffed out his chest and stepped closer to Aki. "What about your shit? Making all these cranes like you can wish away what you did. You're Nao's bitch, and it's starting to seem like you like it up the ass."

Aki's lip curled. If he was Nao's, he wouldn't be angry when people accused him. Aki's muscles tightened, and the veins in his neck twitched. He took a step, pushing Fuse to retreat with sheer presence.

"So what if I do," Aki said. "With one word from me, you'd be done for."

"Like you have any real power in the family. You answer phones. In a year Nao will find some new toy to replace you, and you'll be back to scrubbing floors with me."

From the window, Aki could make out Nao entering the tearoom. Aki needed to prepare the tea. He couldn't keep Nao waiting.

Aki shook his head. "I don't have time for this."

"Don't worry. You'll get all the time you need soon enough."

Aki slammed the door shut behind him and on Fuse's words.

He took in a deep breath at the top of the stairs and didn't let it out until he reached the bottom. He couldn't let his frazzled nerves push their energy into the tea.

It would probably be the last time he'd make tea for Nao, so it had to be perfect.

After Nao had yelled at him for talking to Detective Yamada, Aki had wandered to the historic district. If Nao was going to watch the view from the tearoom at headquarters, Aki could indulge him with sweets to lift his bitter mood. Aki had purchased an egg tart with two bunnies powdered on the top, several rabbit-shaped mochi, and even small dorayaki sweet pancakes shaped to resemble the full moon with bunny packaging. Aki's confection-buying spree had stopped short of buying a hard-boiled egg with pink ears and eyes.

He gathered the sweets and pulled down a pu-erh tea brick. It was flat like a dish and wrapped in white paper with Chinese text marking information about the tea. Aki couldn't read any of it, but he knew the tea had been grown in a few special regions in Yunnan, China.

The cake's earthy aroma transported Aki deep into an ancient forest.

A specific knife needed to be used to break off sections of the disk, and Nao's pu-erh knife was sheathed in red lacquered bamboo. Aki pulled down a smaller teapot because pu-erh could be put through multiple steepings. The flavor of each steeping would be its own journey.

Aki bit his lip and hoped for a wonderful last tea journey with Nao. Aki had never thought much about the different teas before, but since sharing a cup with Nao each morning, his taste buds ignited picking up the nuances of each oxidized oolong.

Nao's tea bowl was easy to pick—the one with the crack sealed with gold—but there were a few left for Aki to pick from.

He held a yellow one, but the shape pushed his hands out too far. The blue one—the texture along the outside reminded Aki of ashen dirt. A splash of green and blue swirled together in the third, creating a maelstrom. It fit the chaos raging inside of him.

Maybe it was silly to put so much effort into the display, but if anyone would notice, it would be Nao.

He grabbed the tray and headed outside. Aki knew he was walking into his death, whether it be from Nao shooting him as he slid open the tearoom door or from rotting in jail. He would be happy to die serving Nao tea.

CHAPTER 15
• • •

"COME IN," Nao called.

Aki slid open the screen door to the traditional tearoom. Exposed wood beams and tatami floor created an escape from the outside world. A wall scroll with a short poem about the moon hung in the tokonoma alcove to ignite the conscience to the season. Aki breathed in the lingering cedar scent while trying to steady the tray, which was growing heavier from guilt.

"Leave the door open so we can see the moon," Nao said.

Nao wore one of his indigo yukata instead of a suit. For him the workday was finished, but it only made the long-sleeved jacket Aki wore more stifling.

"You brought snacks," Nao said.

"They're from the historic district. Since you're unable to see the moon at one of the temples, I humbly thought, perhaps, these would help with the atmosphere."

"You sound so formal."

"Forgive me, I—"

"I'm not going to shoot you if that's where the sudden change comes from."

"I would never think of such…"

"Don't lie to me, Aki." Nao licked his lips.

He leaned forward, placing his hand beside Aki's. Nao's face was centimeters away. Aki didn't deserve to be preparing tea like nothing happened. With all the lies and untold truths, Aki should've been the one to die, not Shoda. Worse still, he couldn't take his eyes off Nao and his all-knowing gaze.

All the pressure released inside Aki as he let out a sharp breath; then all at once, the tears came flooding out. He took off his glasses and rubbed his eyes on the sleeves of his coat, but the tears never stopped.

"I've made… such a horrible mistake," he squeaked out between gasps.

"Don't worry about it right now. Make the tea, then we can talk. You're the only one who can make my tea, remember? So you can do that for me, yes?"

Aki bit back a cry and nodded. Nao leaned back, his palm brushing against Aki's pinkie.

"Good. I knew you could," Nao said. "When I owned a tea shop, and my unwanted thoughts raced through my head, I would make tea and they'd stop. Sometimes I think that was why I opened the shop in the first place. Does making tea have the same effect on you?"

Nao's words washed over Aki like the muffled hum of cicadas, but they were able to ease the pain.

Aki opened his mouth to speak, but his chest grew heavy. Even though the tears had stopped flowing, they'd numbed him. So Aki did only what he could do: make tea.

He unwrapped the tea cake and plunged the sharp knife into it. With a well-placed turn, some leaves separated from the brick. With a few more turns, enough for a pot of tea had been broken off.

A hearth in the center of the room boiled water for the tea, and after heating the pot, Aki dumped the leaves inside. He returned to the formal ceremony, offering Nao one of the sweet treats on a napkin.

Somehow by keeping his full attention on the tea and doing his best to please Nao, Aki was able to shut off thoughts of what was going to happen to him.

"I tried to write some poetry like the nobles used to do," Nao said. "But I'm far from a poet."

"I'm sure you're humbling yourself, Father Murata."

"There you go again, slipping back into formality. No one else is here. I made sure it was just us for a reason."

The last time he had been in the tearoom, Nao had kissed him. It had been a delusion brought on by Nao's fever, but Aki remembered the taste of desire on Nao's lips. Aki clutched his jacket sleeve as Nao tasted the tea.

"Delicious as always," Nao said.

Aki opened his mouth, ready for another formal reply, but closed it. He stared at the deep-caramel-colored tea in his tea bowl. He had to say something, or else his silence would be an admission of guilt. He was guilty, though, and deserved his punishment.

"I enjoy making tea for you and hope I can continue." Aki's voice came just above a whisper.

"You've got to be more careful, then."

"I can—"

"You had a fight. Maybe you can fool the others with your makeup skills, but I know your face well enough to see it was swollen in ways not caused by a boxing glove."

"Shoda attacked me. He was jealous of my—"

"This is where you relax and drink your tea."

Nao asked the impossible, and Aki's eyes widened. He brushed his fingers against the straw floor.

It was real. He was real no matter how much he wished he could disappear. The tea bowl in his other hand was real, too. The speckled texture and smooth glaze mixed with the rough like the bumps and ease of life.

Aki sipped the tea, letting the hot liquid warm his mouth and smooth his muscles.

"Good," Nao said.

Aki smiled and realized how pathetic it was that a single word of encouragement from Nao set him so much at ease. But in the Matsukawa structure, Nao was the only one who mattered.

"You've been so distracted recently. Something had to be on your mind."

Aki nodded and took another sip of tea.

"This should help get your mind off things." Nao reached into his sleeve and pulled out the evidence bag with Aki's crane inside.

"Let me explain," Aki whimpered.

"I know you well enough not to need an explanation. Every expression crossing your face the past few days I've been able to read easier than deciding what tea you'd prepared for me."

Nao leaned back, closing his eyes for a few seconds before gazing up at the moon.

The night still hadn't completely fallen, but the moon glowed.

"It's a wonderful thought," Nao said, "how the moon we are viewing is the same from thousands of years ago, and the same one people thousands of years into the future will see. In the end, none of us matter, but the city has to continue so others have the opportunity to gaze up at the moon and think of all the others who have viewed it for Otsukimi."

The moon was beautiful, and Nao's words made the anguish of the previous nights insignificant. In the end, whatever acts Aki had done were meaningless in respect toward the city.

"I know you wouldn't have allowed things to happen the way they did without a good reason. I've given you numerous opportunities to tell me. Since you haven't, I figured you must think I wouldn't believe you. How could the perfect Matsukawa recruit attack you if you were friends?"

"Forgive my ignorance."

"I don't care about the exact details of how Shoda ended up dead, but I know you wouldn't do anything to endanger this family. You wouldn't cut him in two and leave him to be discovered."

Aki could leap to the moon and carve a love haiku to Nao's trust in the rock. Aki sat up a little straighter while the weight on his chest lessened.

"Thank you," Aki said. "I'm truly humbled by your sentiments, but I'm also an utter failure. I tried to find out where they put Shoda's body, but then it showed up in the lake."

"Of course you wouldn't find it, because someone's trying to frame you. He hid the body where you'd never suspect."

"I don't know who."

"You know exactly who it is." Nao placed the pu-erh knife to Aki's hand. "So make them pay."

The sheathed knife rolled in Aki's palm. "But—"

"Stop trusting people who don't deserve it. You need to show him you do more than answer phones and make tea."

"I—"

Nao curled Aki's fingers around the knife. "You do, and you have the power to show him to never cross you again."

Aki shook his head. "But I can barely fight even with the training."

"Remember when I took you to practice shooting? The first time you hit the target and all the other times you missed?"

"I'm rubbish at shooting, too."

Nao chuckled. "The first time, you didn't know what you were doing and you allowed your instinct told kick in, but then you overthought it. I tried to tell you that when you fought Hiro."

"My instinct?"

"Yes, that's what I do when I fight. I let everything else around me disappear. Nothing else exists but the fight, and there's no thinking it's all pretend."

Aki took in a deep breath. "Pretend like nothing else exists."

Nao squeezed Aki's hand and looked him in the eye. "He's not playing pretend. He wants you dead or jailed. Now make him wish he never dared go against you. I know you can do it."

Aki pressed his lips together, but with Nao's confidence in him, Aki puffed out his chest. The events of the past few days flashed in Aki's mind, and then it came to him. There was only one person who could know what had happened.

"I will fulfill your every desire," Aki said.

He clutched the knife and headed back to headquarters.

CHAPTER 16

· · ·

AKI OPENED HIS bedroom door to find Fuse flipping through a yakuza magazine.

"At least he's not fucking you until you limp anymore, right?" Fuse laughed.

Aki's fingers curled around the sheathed knife. He couldn't overpower Fuse by sheer force, but with Nao's words, Aki could do anything.

"Murata's impossible sometimes." Aki loosened his tie.

"He's not the only one."

Fuse's attention turned back to the magazine. "Have you ever thought of getting a tattoo? Some of these are really badass."

"Yeah?"

Aki let out a shallow breath and with it released all of his thoughts. He couldn't overthink it. Fuse was no friend, just like Shoda hadn't been when he turned on Aki.

He balled his hand into a fist and whacked the side of Fuse's head. It might've been a cheap shot, but Nao had made it clear cheap shots didn't exist in a real fight.

Fuse moaned, his movements lagging with disorientation. Aki landed another punch to Fuse's face. A dull ache swelled in Aki's knuckles, but with the numbing adrenaline pumping to every muscle, it didn't slow him down.

Aki pulled off his tie and restrained Fuse's hands behind his back. It was a lot easier than firing a gun, especially with Fuse still in shock.

"W-what are you doing?" Fuse mumbled.

Then Fuse's legs flew up from under Aki and kicked the side of his leg. Aki fumbled to the ground, knocking over the basket full of cranes. The knife rolled out of his hand and into the paper.

"What the fuck are you doing!" Fuse yelled.

Aki lunged forward before Fuse could get to his feet. Aki's muscles burned as he put his full weight onto Fuse's knees to keep them still.

"Get off me, you homo."

Thoughts would ebb up in Aki's mind, but he followed Nao's advice and ignored them. Aki unfastened his belt, grabbed the buckled end, and flung the rest out of his belt loops. He secured Fuse's feet together. Fuse tried to kick, but Aki lay on his legs, so he only flopped around like a fish out of water.

"Get off me," Fuse groaned.

"Not after what you did."

"What are you going to do? Fuck me?"

"More like fuck you up," Aki hissed and grabbed the knife amongst the fallen cranes. "You and Shoda were so jealous of my position you were going to attack me?"

"I don't know what you're talking about."

"I think you do."

Fuse thrashed, but since he was tied up, it did little to throw off Aki.

Aki unsheathed the knife and held it up to Fuse's throat. "Tell me what you guys had planned."

"We were supposed to join up again and just kick the crap out of you, honestly. Shoda was the one who got all crazy and brought a knife."

"Funny, I got one right here."

"But there are no hard feelings between us, right?"

Aki drew a thin red line on Fuse's neck with the blade.

"There's definitely some hard feelings," Aki said. "How could you even do that to Shoda's body?"

"You're the one who stuffed him in the trunk and let him die there."

"He was dead before I put him in there!"

"Oh."

Aki narrowed his eyes. Fuse put everything Aki held dear in jeopardy because he couldn't be bothered to check if Shoda was dead. How dare he think Aki didn't care about his friendship with Shoda enough to let him die! Even after he attacked him, Aki wouldn't have been so heartless.

"I was going to deal with him when I had time."

"Fine, I made a mistake. Can you get up?"

Aki laughed. "You were trying to frame me!"

"I thought you let him die in your trunk. You would've deserved something for that."

"What you did would've gotten the whole family in trouble. How could you not see? If you really had an issue, you should've gone directly to Father Murata."

"And tell him his fuck toy killed the best recruit."

"I'm not his fuck toy. I'm his secretary," Aki said between clenched teeth.

"Fine. You talk to Murata since you can reason with him."

"You should be able to speak with the head of the family before you chop one of us up."

"Let me go, Aki. This isn't like you."

Aki shook his head. Nao expected him to make Fuse pay for what he had done. It came as a direct order, and there was no backing out of it. Nao's words gave Aki a strength he didn't know he possessed.

"You've always thought of yourself, but that's going to change today. You'll always have to think about the family every time you look at your stupid face," Aki said.

"Come on, Aki, we're friends. I won't do anything like that again. I promise."

"Friends?"

"Yeah, we were friends since you joined."

"Friends don't try to kill each other."

Aki took in a deep breath and gathered up his strength. Nao's words echoed in Aki's ears louder than Fuse's pleas. His words slurred when Aki pushed Fuse's face to the floor.

Everything disappeared.

Fuse trembled underneath Aki's weight, and Aki could imagine Nao cheering him on. Aki's grip tightened on the knife, and he pressed it against Fuse's cheek, carving the inward-facing arrows of the Matsukawa crest.

Fuse screamed and tried to shake, but Aki pressed his arms on Fuse's head to hold it steady.

Aki went over the mark a few times to make sure the scar would stay forever.

When it was over, Aki stood. "You can never find a job anywhere else. You have to spend your whole life serving the Matsukawa. So for the first time, you can't think of yourself first."

Aki left the bedroom, carrying the bloody knife with him.

CHAPTER 17
• • •

AKI STEPPED OUT of the tub and toweled himself off. It had only been a few hours since he'd carved the Matsukawa crest into Fuse's cheek, but Aki's muscles ached like tree pulp being pressed into paper.

Nao had everyone in the house waiting outside Aki and Fuse's bedroom. When the deed was done and Aki left the room, Nao applauded, and then everyone else followed. The attention had made Aki's body grow hot. Yet during Aki's bath, it hadn't been the praise from the household he played over and over, but how hard Nao laughed when he'd seen Fuse's face.

Thinking about Nao always left Aki tingling, but knowing he'd made Nao so happy sent lightning through each nerve. Alone in the bathroom, he could find some release.

Aki sighed and pulled on his robe. Perhaps one day Nao would get over whatever was blocking him and act on the desire Aki knew was there. It would be impossible to tell how long Nao would take.

"Where are you going?" Nao asked, as Aki took a few steps down the hall.

Aki hadn't taken his glasses into the bath, so Nao's face was blurred. But Aki couldn't miss Nao's smile or the lax way his obi secured his yukata and exposed more of his chest than usual.

"Was there something you needed, Father Murata?" Aki brushed back his damp hair.

"I'm impressed how you handled Fuse."

Aki bowed his head, but it couldn't hide his smile. "You humble me with your compliment. I don't deserve praise, especially with regards to that situation."

"It was perfect." Nao licked his lips. "You knew we need all the recruits we can get, so you didn't kill him. You forced him to put the family before himself. Now everyone who meets Fuse will see what you are capable of. You have your own story protecting you."

Nao tugged at his yukata, exposing more of his sharp collarbone. Aki swallowed his arousal.

"You going back to your room?" Nao asked.

"Unless I can be of service to you."

"It's just you're going the wrong way."

Aki arched an eyebrow.

"Your room's there now." Nao pointed to the door beside his bedroom. "I had the recruits move your things while you bathed."

Aki's cheeks grew warm, and he swallowed before speaking. "Thank you."

"You don't have to share it, and since it's a corner room, I'll be your only neighbor. It should help with the light-sleeping problem. If people on the stairs bother you, tell me and I'll speak to the lead feets personally."

Aki couldn't keep the smile off his face. To be able to share a wall with Nao each night was too much for what he deserved.

"I was curious how many cranes you had left. So I had them counted. You're one away from a thousand," Nao said.

"That's the most I've made in such a short amount of time."

"Do you know what you want to wish for?"

"Not yet."

Nao took a step closer and picked a stray hair off Aki's robe.

"Whatever it is you wish for, make it something good," Nao whispered in his ear then wandered off with a seductive grin on his face.

Aki shook his head. It had to be his imagination. He stepped into his new room. It wasn't as big as his old one, but he didn't have to share it. His few possessions were clustered together on the hardwood floor, and the suits Nao had given him hung in the closet. Aki put away his dirty clothes and slipped on his glasses.

The moon rose higher in the night sky, and the noises of the house softened. Nao's bedroom door opened and closed, and the soft murmurs of him talking to Nobu came through the wall before subsiding in what had to be Nao's slumber.

The basket of cranes sat to the side of his things. Nine were lined up outside with a single red square of paper at the end.

Aki sat and began folding the last of a thousand cranes. They were all for him, and it was up to him to make a wish deserving of each one.

He took longer on the final crane than any before, pressing down each crease with his fingernail and perfectly aligning the folds. The final crane came to life in sixteen folds he'd done a thousand times before. He pressed a hand against his shared bedroom wall and held the crane to his heart.

Aki wished for nothing but to remain by Nao's side.

◆ ◆ ◆

Look for

THE DEAFENING SILENCE

book 4 of

THE YAKUZA PATH

series coming out in Winter 2018.

As a gift, enjoy the first chapter of Amy's
other series, Would It Be Okay to Love You?

ABOUT THE AUTHOR

· · ·

AMY TASUKADA LIVES in North Texas with a calico cat called O'Hara. As an only child her day dreams kept her entertained, and at age ten she started to put them to paper. Since then her love of writing hasn't ceased. She can be found drinking hot tea and filming Japanese street fashion hauls on her YouTube channel.

CONNECT WITH AMY ON…
Website: AmyTasukada. com
Facebook: Facebook. com/amytasukadaofficial
Twitter: Twitter. com/amytasukada
Youtube: YouTube. com/user/amytasukada

AN ANIME FANBOY. AN EROTIC VOICE ACTOR. WILL THEIR SECRET OVERWHELM THEIR LOVE?

◆ ● ◆

Sato doesn't get out much. The anime company accountant spends his days at a desk and his nights working on his own small-scale robots. His geeky life is like a dream, but it has just one piece missing…

The world only knows Aoi for his moans. The erotic voice actor of boys' love dramas has legions of fangirls obsessed with his gasps of simulated ecstasy. And his new boyfriend Sato can barely handle the attention.

As Aoi's popularity rises and secrets about his past begin to reveal themselves, can the accountant and the voice actor rise above their problems to create something real?

To start reading this lighthearted love story today, simply sign up for Amy Tasukada's newsletter for this monthly slice-of-life romance. A new short is sent every month!

Sign up for your free story at
WWW. AMYTASUKADA. COM

WOULD IT BE OKAY
TO LOVE YOU?

AMY TASUKADA

CHAPTER 1

SATO PLANTED HIMSELF in the middle of the do-it-yourself Gundam robot model kits. He could rattle off the names of each robot figure with a single glance and could whip up an Excel presentation about the anime series within minutes. But today he frowned because the bright-colored boxes offered nothing new.

He pushed up his dark-rimmed glasses with a sigh and moved along the aisle. With the three-day vacation, he needed something to occupy his time besides binge-watching old anime DVDs and eating vending machine snacks.

Sato jerked as he bumped into a teenager who apparently shared his love of model kits.

"Sorry." He took a step back. "I didn't see you there."

The teenager waved off the apology with a smile. He had to be the shortest person Sato had ever seen outside of primary school, but Sato loomed over everyone he met, so he wasn't the right person to judge. Sato had started assembling the kits when he was around the teen's age, which probably added to his having trouble finding a new one. Smiling back, Sato resumed his search.

The first soft strings of Beethoven's Ninth Symphony played over the anime shop's speakers. Even in Sato's favorite store he couldn't escape the holiday song.

"I can't believe they're playing this song here," the teen said. "I'll be glad when the New Year's over so I don't have to hear it for another eleven months."

A fit of giggles erupted from the checkout line, cutting off any reply Sato would've given—not that he'd planned on giving one to the teen.

Sato peeked over the robot display and caught a look at the group of laughing women. They all clutched the same CD. No major anime soundtracks had dropped today, but Sato only kept track of Gundam releases or the series he did the accounting for. It was probably for some magical girl anime release.

He ignored their laughter from there and went back to searching for kits. He had New Year's money to spend.

After a few more minutes of searching, Sato found two model kits worthy of assembling. He liked one figure more, but the other would be more challenging. After all, he couldn't spend his entire New Year's vacation watching anime like last year.

"It's really hard to pick one sometimes, isn't it?" Sato said.

"I guess so," the teenager said.

Sato bit his lip. Usually he wouldn't hold a conversation with random strangers, but the teen clearly loved Gundam as much as he did. Why else would he linger as much as he had?

The teenager lifted his sunglasses and perched them on his black beanie. Blond hair peeked out from under the hat. He smiled at Sato, showing the dimples on his cheeks.

"They let you dye your hair in school now?" Sato blurted out without thinking. "A friend of mine got in trouble when he lightened his to brown."

"I'm twenty-five."

"Oh, please excuse me, I didn't mean…" Sato bit his lip.

"Is it because I'm short?" The dimples disappeared, and a mischievous glint appeared in the man's green eyes. "Maybe you're just really tall."

"Sorry."

"Don't worry so much. I once bought my friend a pack of cigarettes and a cop popped out of nowhere and said I was too young to use the vending machine. He went into this big lecture, then I showed him my ID and he thought it was a fake! He threatened to call my parents and everything."

Sato gave a weary smile and rubbed the back of his neck. Knowing the blond was close to his own age zapped away what little social courage he possessed.

The man's gaze met Sato's, then wandered down his body without shame. Sato's face grew hot, and his heart thumped in his ears.

"So is everything else about you as big?" he asked.

"I—ah…"

The guy was actually flirting with him? Sato's technique consisted of vaguely making eye contact and hoping the other person realized he was into him. The way the blond's crooked smile spread across his face didn't make Sato's heart beat any quieter.

In the accounting department, the most out-there anyone got was wearing a khaki suit. Sato had never even talked to anyone bold enough to wear colored contacts and dye their hair so drastically. He pushed up his glasses but couldn't squeak out a reply.

"So which one did you decide on getting?" the blond asked.

Sato swallowed. The man still wanted to hold a conversation with him?

"I think this one." Sato picked a five-hour do-it-yourself kit. It would take him three if he was lucky.

"Nice choice."

Sato rubbed his sweaty palms against his coat. "I—ah—which one are you getting?"

"Oh, these."

He held up a few manga graphic novels. The cover of one had a man clinging onto another man, his private parts covered by a conveniently placed bedsheet. They were boys' love novels. Sato's tongue twisted into a Windsor knot like his tie.

If the guy was reading them, then he surely had to be gay, or at least bi. Though the fact he'd flirted with Sato had to be the biggest giveaway.

Sato's breath caught in his throat even thinking of buying a gay manga himself.

Sure he'd dated people who were out before. There'd been that upperclassman in high school, but that had only lasted three days. His college boyfriend had lasted longer. They'd been in the same trigonometry class and had even studied together. Then he'd stopped taking Sato's calls after the final exam. Sato tugged at his tie. He couldn't really count those as meaningful relationships.

The man stared at Sato.

"So you're not getting a kit?" Sato asked.

"I ducked here to hide from them." The blond pointed to the door where the group of women walked out.

"All of them?"

He laughed. "What can I say?"

Heading to the boys' love section with a gaggle of boyX-boy-crazed women would have any man running to avoid their questions. The blond was cute, too, so they probably would've wanted to snap a photo.

"Well, ah—" Sato cleared his throat. "Nice talking to you."

Sato knew when he was defeated and walked to the checkout line. The blond was so different from the guys at the accounting office that Sato couldn't carry on any more of a conversation. His words tangled in his mouth like adding-machine paper on tax day.

Sato rubbed the corner of the cardboard box. Once he cracked it open, he'd forget all about the man.

The last woman left, and only nerds like Sato were left in line. Outside of events, the anime store rarely got busy, but with New Year's everyone had extra cash to spend.

The blond got in line behind him, and the ball of nerves in Sato twisted tighter. Normal people could have conversations with people who flirted with them, but all Sato could do was gnaw on his bottom lip and look like the biggest loser ever. No wonder his Gundam robot collection outnumbered the people he interacted with. He'd seem like a bigger idiot if he didn't at least attempt to say something… anything.

The music switched to an anime theme that Sato recognized. It wasn't something he really watched, but it was popular.

"This anime is everywhere," Sato pushed out. "Almost as bad as the Ninth Symphony and New Year's."

"That's for sure." The blond laughed, and it lit up Sato's world.

"Have you listened to the soundtrack for the Mobile Suit Gundam? That's my favorite of all of them."

It was a classic.

"I admit I've never watched anything Gundam."

How could anyone not watch Gundam? Sato cocked an eyebrow. "Really? None at all?"

"Parents wouldn't let me watch TV."

Not being able to talk about robots killed most of the topics Sato could talk about.

"What soundtracks do you like, then?" Sato asked.

"If I had to choose, there's an anime called Gravitation. I liked that soundtrack," the blond said. "Maybe more how they put the album together than the songs themselves."

"Oh, I've never heard of it."

"It was about this rock star and a writer and their relationship. They had a real musician sing all the songs, so it was fun. They didn't really match the voices that well, though."

"The voices didn't match?"

"The singer had a distinct singing voice so when the voice actor was acting his lines it was a little hard to believe they were the same person. They tried, but you could tell."

Sato shrugged. "I guess they should've had the singer say the character lines."

"Then you end up with someone who can't really act. Like when they get athletes to play roles in movies."

They moved up in line, and the blond pointed to a CD by the checkout. "That one's pretty good."

It had two guys on the cover and looked like one of those slow coming-of-age stories. They always had relaxing soundtracks, so it could make for something good to listen to while he assembled the robot.

Sato reached the counter and placed the CD on top of the model kit.

"I hope you like it." The blond winked.

The store clerk rang up Sato's purchases; then Sato nodded a goodbye to the blond and walked out.

The cold chill hit his face, and a light dusting of snow floated down from the sky before disappearing as it hit the ground. Sato headed home, but with each step he took his thoughts remained on the guy he'd left behind. He had to at least know his name.

Sato stopped.

He'd never been so curious about someone in his life. Maybe he could ask him more about the soundtrack, then slip in the name question. If his tongue didn't get tied into a dozen knots first.

The blond walked out of the store, his sunglasses pulled over his green eyes. He stuffed his hands into the pockets of his jacket, that looked way too thin for the Tokyo winter. The guy was so tiny he had to be freezing. His butt did look really nice in those jeans, though.

"Wait," Sato called, coming to his senses.

With Sato's long legs, he caught up with the man quickly.

"Hey, we just met at the anime store," Sato said. "I—I guess you remember, since it just happened."

Could he be any lamer?

"What's up, big boy?"

Sato cleared his throat. "What I mean to say is—ah. What's your name?"

The man raised an eyebrow. "Only my name?"

"If that's okay? I know we just met and you're not into Gundam—"

"Aoi," he interrupted. "My name is Aoi."

Sato blinked. The man gave his first name. It was way too informal for just meeting.

"I mean, what's your surname?"

"It's just Aoi."

"Well, Aoi." Sato's cheeks grew hot. "You can call me Sato."

"Nice to meet you, Sato. I hope for your favor in the coming year."

The mix of informality with Sato being able to say Aoi's first name and then the formal happy New Year's wish threw Sato off so much that he missed Aoi walking off. Sato already looked like a fool; there was no reason to make it worse by looking like a creepy stalker.

Sato sighed. It wasn't like Aoi would be the kind of guy that would want to hang out with him anyway. At least he had the model to get his mind off what a failure he was at picking up guys.

BUY THE BOOK TO GET YOUR OWN LOVE COLLECTIBLE TODAY!

WWW. AMYTASUKADA. COM/WOULD-IT